RETURN TO AYLFORTH

Return to Aylforth

A NOVEL OF SUSPENSE

BY *Anne Eliot* •

•

MEREDITH PRESS • *New York*

RETURN TO AYLFORTH

1

I stopped the car in a turnout on the back lane. In a few minutes I would drive properly to the front entrance of Aylforth Priory, but now I needed to follow one of my old traditions and go first to the remnant of the old abbey that for so many years of my childhood had been a favorite refuge. A little respite was needed before I faced the house and the people—those who were there and those who weren't.

In the misty silence of the lane I heard a thrush; somewhere a horse was trotting behind me. Then, ahead, from the belt of trees, came men's voices. None of those would interfere with my sentimental pilgrimage. I left the car and started toward the gap in the stone wall. From beyond the thick row of hawthorn a voice said decisively, "One to watch inside and one out. That was the arrangement." Another voice said, "Stop. Someone . . ."

As I reached the gap a tall young man, darkly handsome, in city clothes, stepped through it and confronted me. "Can you tell me the way to the village?" he asked.

His voice was pleasant. "My car has given out. I thought I might find a shortcut." He nodded vaguely to the path.

"The only way to the village is to follow this lane as it curves around and then take the right fork," I told him. "It's not more than a mile."

He bent down a little. Behind us on the lane the horse trotted past at an unbroken pace. "Thank you. I'll just start walking, then." He touched the brim of his hat and moved away down the lane. I crossed the wall and glanced in both directions, but there was no sign of the other man who had been speaking.

At first the encounter, slight as it was, put me out of my nostalgic mood. After all, I had been away from Aylforth, except for those short visits, for a long time. My stay would not be long now. I must forget about the past. But the calm of the beech wood was so soothing, the glimpse of the little glade so unchanged, that when I came into the open, where the grass swept down to the gray walls, my heart caught in my throat.

What was left of the old abbey—two low walls forming a small corner and the remnant of an arch—lay at the edge of the rectangle that had once been the refectory. By some lost tradition it had always been kept in grass that grew thicker and greener with the centuries. Across the rectangle stretched orchards, fields, more woods, and, to the right, toward the house, the kitchen gardens. The walled garden, with its pleached fruit trees and beds of berries, came next; the rose garden and a yew walk lay beside the house. Bluff King Hal, about whom there are as many opinions as there are people who have bothered to think about him, had turned Aylforth Priory over to one of the Langlades, a minor courtier—it was a minor foundation anyway—who had built his house from the stones and settled his family into a pleasant and long-lasting possession. It had been home to me for all my childhood.

But it had not been home for these last seven years, and with Cousin Aylmer gone, it seemed unlikely I would ever live here again. There was one treasure from the past I would take with me. I walked around the broken arch and knelt by the inner wall. The ivy was thick and tenacious, but I disturbed only a few tendrils. I took out my nail file and began to work at the third stone, second in, from the arch. It would not move, though I loosened it around all the edges, and I gave a sob of frustration. Suddenly it had become very important to retrieve my treasure. I would keep it as a talisman. I found a sliver of broken rock and pried with that, and at last the stone moved enough for me to grip the edges and pull it out. Eagerly I reached in the hole and drew out a small package wrapped in cloth. I must restore the piece of the wall before I looked—that was part of the original ritual when I had come there for comfort years ago—but by this time my knees hurt from crouching and I sat down on the fallen stone imbedded in the turf.

Slowly I unwound the piece of silver-protecting cloth I had begged from Nanny: there was my box, still shining and gay. It was small and square, with two raised dragons rearing at each other on the lid and chasing around the sides. For as long as this treasure stayed hidden I had been sure I would return to Aylforth. Now I would take it back to London with me. As I looked at the dear dragons and felt the silver begin to warm to my touch, I suddenly began to cry for all that was gone—my childhood, kind Nanny, Cousin Aylmer who had sheltered me. It was a long time since I had cried, but I was tired from weeks of exacting work in the city. The tears were a comfort.

"Do you realize you are trespassing? Are you lost?" The voice above me was cold and clipped and definitely unfriendly. "Or are you overcome by the sight of ruins? There is a ruined castle, open to the public, less than a mile away, far more worthy of your emotions."

I gulped and reached in my bag for a handkerchief. As I mopped my eyes anger rose within me. Trespassing? I? On Aylforth land? How dare anyone say that to me? I knew, even now, every foot of the place as no new gamekeeper or gardener could. I looked up, ready to blast such impertinence.

The man was no gamekeeper. He was tall and lean, with deep-brown hair and gray eyes and surprisingly thick black lashes. His face was tanned, the chin firm, the mouth well shaped. The right eyebrow was broken by a narrow diagonal scar. Mist had covered the tweed jacket with droplets that shone like diamonds. Authority lay in the very set of the shoulders.

I brushed back my hair from my face. "You have no right to speak to me like that," I said as quietly as I could.

The movement had shown the silver box in my lap. I saw him look at that, at me, at the hole in the wall. A lean brown hand swooped down and picked up my box. "Not just trespass but theft also?" he inquired. "Are the tears because there is no more silver in the hole for you to take? You're the second stranger I've seen on the land within the last half hour, and I don't like it."

Return to Aylforth 6

I struggled to my feet. "That box is mine. And there never was anything else in the wall but a white pebble."

The jagged eyebrow rose in disbelief. "A likely story! But you came to steal this, obviously. I'll take charge of it."

I opened my mouth to explain, but as his gray glance swept over me and dismissed me, he interrupted. "Don't try to get out of it. You knew the box was there—I wonder how—and you came and got it. I'll escort you off the property."

"I'll go as I came," I told him furiously. I picked up my bag. The box was loose in his hand. "Look in the hole there and see if there isn't a white pebble."

"That would prove nothing," he said flatly, but he stooped and thrust his left hand into the hollow. As he did so I snatched the box and ran along the lichened wall to the woods. If he followed me I could lose him. At the beeches I glanced over my shoulder. He was standing by the wall, watching; he wouldn't follow—no doubt he felt it beneath his dignity. As the path turned I slowed down and wondered who he was. Some guest at the house, probably, or even a new, overly protective neighbor.

The beech woods seemed more dim than before as I hastened through them. I remembered how we used to frighten ourselves, and each other, running there at dusk as we played robbers and highwaymen. A pheasant clucked, and farther in the distance a stick snapped. I was glad to get back to my Austin. I noticed there was no disabled car in the lane. I rubbed the box against my cheek, put it in my bag, and began to drive slowly to the left fork and so to the gates of the drive.

Even as a child it had always given me pleasure to

look at Aylforth Priory from where the woods fell back and the lawn swept down from the front terrace. The house was all Tudor, gray stone, spreading, gabled, well chimneyed above the main house and also the wings, which ran back to make the courtyard and stables. I swung around the fountain and to the left to take the car to the rear. There was no space provided in front of Aylforth Priory for cars to park and mar the effect.

Two cars were in the garage opposite the stables. Though there was plenty of space for the Austin, I set it next the wall of the kitchen garden, where I could move it easily, left my bag, and walked over the cobblestones to the door that led to the back entry and the corridor to the drawing room. Beneath the gray sky the house looked chill and not as welcoming as I remembered it.

Well, it probably wouldn't be welcoming without Cousin Aylmer. He had cared for me as if I were his own and not just the orphan of distant cousins he had loved and lost, cared for me over Cousin Eugenia's protests and included a good school at the right time, too. But it was the happy childhood I remembered with longing, the years that were sunny in spite of everything. Tears were near the surface, but I blinked them back and lifted my chin. No, I wouldn't be welcome. Eugenia and Isabelle had never liked me, and they wouldn't be glad to see me, although it was only respect that brought me to Cousin Aylmer's memorial service. Respect and an affection I wished I had expressed more openly and by more than occasional brief visits.

The black door with the tiny leaded panes swung open easily. I had never rung at any door at Aylforth; I wasn't starting now. Ahead, pale light from the courtyard windows showed the facing doors in the corridor closed. At the end lay the jog to the front hall, the sweeping staircase and the wide front doors. There were voices in the drawing room. It was so familiar that my youthful uncertainties began to take over. I shook myself and told myself I was no longer the child who could be made to feel gawky and homely and barely tolerated. In London I had learned I was adequately attractive, and I had made myself into a person who could hold her own among enemies and friends. I must not let even the Priory and its people swamp that knowledge. Besides, I was here by right, because of Cousin Aylmer and Nanny. Quickly I turned into the room.

Cousin Eugenia sat in the high-backed green brocade chair behind the tea table, just as she had for years. The lamp beside her made a circle around the china and silver and left her face in shadow. Isabelle, more blondly beautiful than ever, was on the sofa that faced the wide fireplace and small fire. A tall young man by the mantel sipped his tea and watched her, of course.

"There is practically no family remaining," Cousin Eugenia was saying in that voice that always seemed to be whining even when it wasn't. "But all the county will come tomorrow, no matter what the weather."

"Thinking over the remnants of the family," said Isabelle, "I doubt if any of them know about it, or turn up."

"Here's one who has," I said briskly before my heart failed me. "Cousin Eugenia, how are you?" I skirted the couch and kissed lightly the cheek nearest me. I like to keep up appearances when possible.

"Pér-dita!" Cousin Eugenia always called me by my

. . . . 9

full name when she was displeased. "You did not send word you were coming."

"Only knew about the service when I saw the paper this morning. No one had told me about it." I returned around the couch and sat down at the other end from Isabelle.

"We didn't think you'd be interested," Isabelle said coolly. "It's three years since you were here, isn't it?"

"Two, for a visit," I answered gently. "You always did exaggerate, Isabelle."

She smiled, but there was not enough light to see the expression in her eyes. "You remember Roger Daintry, Perdita?" She looked at the young man.

"Of course." He did not much resemble the Roger who used to play with us, but vaguely I could see the child in the adult's face.

A teacup clicked gently. "Yes, I would like some tea, thank you," I remarked to the room. "Milk and one sugar, please."

Roger brought it to me, and I had an impression of brown face and hair and eyes and tweed.

"I don't see really why you came," Cousin Eugenia complained fretfully.

There were many things I could have said, and I was mildly proud of myself that I said none of them. "Is the house so full there's no room?" I asked instead.

"Of course there's room, and of course you won't be staying long anyway."

"I might . . ." I began, just to annoy her.

"Why not let Perdita have the nursery," interposed Isabelle smoothly. "She would feel at home there. Then there would be no problem however long she stayed."

"Lovely," I agreed brightly. Score for Isabelle. She

knew how ghosts would haunt the corners of the room and no Nanny there for comfort.

"Your car's in the back? I'll take up your bag." Roger hurried away.

Cousin Eugenia rose, a trifle stiffly, and swept to the door, her long skirts making a slurring sound over the rugs. "It's an hour and a half to the first gong," she remarked. "No doubt you are tired and will wish to rest."

I wasn't quite that tired, but I was glad of the dismissal. I had no desire to cope with Isabelle at the moment, though I would have liked to ask her what happened to her last two engagements.

We three had reached the hall when there came the swish that only a Rolls can make on gravel as it rounds a curve.

"Now, who?" began Eugenia to me as though I were responsible.

When the doorbell gonged, a new butler moved from the back hall to the front door, opened it, and stood aside. In swept an imposing figure who could only be Cousin Alexandra. I couldn't help smiling with pleasure. There were other figures behind her.

"Eugenia!" Her voice was as mellow and charming as ever. "You fox! You might have let me know about the service. But you were always sly. Poor Aylmer. Of course I came. Isabelle, Perdita . . ." Her hat, rows of tulle and one rose, nodded at us. "Sloane." She did not have to turn; the chauffeur, laden with Vuitton cases, was beside her. "Carry all that to the second floor. Then you can return to the inn in the village. Mrs. Langlade feels the fewer the better. Which room, Eugenia? The blue?"

"That is mine now," Eugenia told her flatly. "The

green will be even more convenient for you. It will be made ready immediately. Manson, please tell Susan to hurry with the rooms.''

''And the nursery, Mother,'' put in Isabelle.

Before Manson could murmur his ''Yes, madam,'' Alexandra swung back into action. ''You really should have sent me a message, Eugenia, about the memorial service. And I even had to read in the papers about dear Aylmer's death, nearly a month ago, and that the memorial service would be later.''

''He wanted everything very quiet.'' Eugenia, in exasperation, raised her voice to an unaccustomed pitch. ''First cremation and no funeral and then a service no sooner than a month after. I thought the notice in the paper sufficient for anyone interested.''

Alexandra surveyed her blandly. ''I should have thought the heir—''

''He was not yet here. I arranged everything.'' Her mouth tightened in defiance and her gaze shifted. ''Who's that behind you?''

''Ah, yes. We'll need another room for the two young men. One is here.'' She gestured, and a towering blond young man appeared at her side. ''I've brought Amaury de Montluc along. After all, he's a cousin, too, though distant, and Aylmer did take in the Princess and her boys when they escaped from France. Nico came on ahead and should be here any moment, if he hasn't lost his way.''

Amaury kissed Cousin Eugenia's hand. ''It is so long I could not expect you to remember,'' he said gently and then smiled at all of us, a nice open smile in a broad face that looked more Magyar than French. ''Isabelle,

Petra." His eyes were a bright light blue and there was color under the tanned skin. "I had hoped you would be here."

"Only proper the boys should come," took up Cousin Alexandra. "Also, they want to see if the missing pictures could be here."

"We have heard . . . but they couldn't be . . ." Cousin Eugenia was nearly fluttering.

"We'll find out later. We've had tea, Eugenia, thank you. We'd better all go to our rooms now. Is it seven for cocktails? Amaury, your arm." But I noticed that she went up the stairs without leaning on it.

"Well!" exploded Eugenia. "She always was high-handed, but . . . I must talk to Mrs. Mellowfield." She hurried away as though to avoid us both.

Isabelle and I glanced at each other. "You're looking well," she said vaguely, so I knew I wasn't. "You remember the way?"

"I do. And you're looking very handsome yourself." She always brought out the worst in me; she had never cared for the adjective "handsome." We nodded, and I went up to the long hall and the nursery at the far corner.

The low, wainscoted room was dearly familiar. No one had troubled to change it. The center window still squeaked as I pushed it open to look down the terrace to the oaks. My favorite view. How many characters had I pretended to be as I sat here! There was so much to remember . . . if I let myself.

The ladder-back chair and footstool still stood at an angle to the center window. If I looked, quickly, surely I would see Nanny there, erect, in the soft blue she always wore because that was the color the Princess preferred, sewing while she waited for us, or listening as we talked by the fire. I should have come back to do her errands quickly, but she had said in that ghost of her comfortable voice, "There's no hurry, Petra. Just a few things to take to some people. The list is in the trunk, and that, as I've said, is in the back attic. You're a busy young lady, and we both know why you don't come down very often. Just take care of it all for me when next you visit." Well, there *had* been reasons for my delay. . . .

A knock stopped that first backward look. "It's Susan, miss," said the cheerful-looking, rather plump girl when I opened the door. "To make your bed." She rushed an armful of linen and blankets toward it. "I should dust, too, miss. We only do it once a week." In spite of the brightness she looked harried.

"Put all that on the chest," I told her. "I'll make the bed, and you can dust, if you have a chance, while we're at dinner. I'm sure you must have a lot to do now."

"Oh, I have, miss, what with Lady Harborne coming this way all of a sudden and the room for the two gentlemen to do. But I'll come back later, miss, thank you." She practically ran from the room.

First I took out my rescued silver box, stroked the dragons and opened it, to let out the old troubles, then wrapped it in a handkerchief and stowed it behind the cornice of the wardrobe, in case Cousin Eugenia took to prying. Then I unpacked and made the bed quickly so there'd be time for a tub. Fortunately, with the vague idea of going on to Devon for a rest and change, I'd brought enough clothes for at least two weeks. Would the blue dinner dress be all right? Cousin Aylmer had never liked black—he used to call the women who wore it black crows. Yes, I'd always looked well in blue, and I loved chiffon that swirled around my feet.

As I soaked I began to relax, and to remember. The silver box had brought back so much. It was when I was getting over the measles that Cousin Aylmer gave it to me. He had come on one of his after-tea visits and found me recovering and irritable and proclaiming I was going to get up. His long kind face had regarded me gravely for a moment, then he put his hand in his pocket and brought out this box. "I found this yesterday," he said calmly, "and it made me think of you. Here, it is a bribe. If you will stay in bed two more days, it is yours. See, you can put all your troubles inside, and the dragons on the lid will keep them there, away from you. And you can change the troubles as you wish."

Awed, nodding agreement, I held out my hands. I had never owned anything so lovely; the silver shone, the dragons looked as if they were moving. I looked up to say "Thank you" and found his blue eyes sympathetic and amused, and on impulse I stood up in bed and put my arms around his neck. "I'll keep it forever," I whispered as I kissed him.

"You may, after two days," he promised.

Of course Cousin Eugenia spotted it on the table by my bed on her next brief visit. She picked it up. "This is much too valuable for you to play with. Where did you get it?"

I took it from her and told her. She sniffed. "Aylmer should not have done that. It is old, a patch box, I believe, Chinese and good. I will take care of it for you when you are well."

. . . . 15

I knew that meant I would never see it again, so I kept my lovely box hidden in my room, changing the hiding place often. Once she asked for it when Cousin Aylmer was away, but Nanny diverted her. It was then I knew I must hide it well. Months before I had been looking for buried treasure and found a stone in the arch of the ruin that moved and there I had left a white pebble behind it for good luck. Now my wrapped box went in beside the pebble. For several years after that I would come and open the box and tell the dragons my troubles had changed and they must take care of new ones, and I used to think it worked. Later I would come just for the pleasure of looking at it. When I left for London, it had stayed behind, the one thing that was mine at Aylforth.

The Priory had always seemed home to me. Now, in spite of my sad reasons for coming, it was good to be here again. Inevitably things would change. I wondered who was the heir. I had never heard . . . due to some family quarrel, I recalled vaguely. Cousin Aylmer would not be one to talk of quarrels, or heirs, and Cousin Eugenia would not be one to acknowledge the possibility of any alteration in her comfortable way of life. It would be some very distant cousin, I supposed. Would he let the family come back to visit occasionally? Suddenly I hated the thought of leaving Aylforth forever. But perhaps he was already bringing in his own people—that man by the ruin, for instance. He had talked as if he knew the place. I'd find out a good deal at dinner, for Alexandra would be curious, and she had never had any inhibitions about asking questions. And what about this Amaury de Montluc? He was coming back from the past. Of course, the Montluc boys and the Princess had come with Nanny from France that other June, when I had been a shy and desolate five-year-old, keeping to myself in this strange new world. Now, in some ways, it might be strange again.

2

    As I went down the stairs it was as if I had never been away.

Aylforth Priory remained as it had begun, a simple Tudor house. It was no Knole or Hardwick. A quadrangle, it had been built around a courtyard that was bordered and crisscrossed by flagged walks edged with low box. In the center was a fountain where a decorous marble putto was clutching a dolphin, brought back from some forgotten grand tour. Some Langlade had turned the gate house into an entrance hall with a paving of black and white squares of marble, a wide staircase that mounted on three sides, and a skylight above. Another, perhaps he who had done nicely under the second Charles, had installed a tremendous chandelier, gilt-framed mirrors and marble-topped tables, and a later one had made some of the little rooms into big ones.

On the left of the hall, as one entered from the parterre, was the drawing room, with French windows to the front and on either side of the fireplace at the far end. The morning room was next, at right angles, and then the library and last Cousin Aylmer's study. Across the entrance hall the dining room repeated the pattern, with pantry, kitchen, storeroom and estate office beyond. A low hall ran between the courtyard and the two rows of rooms. On the far side of the square reared a two-story banqueting hall that no one had ever been able to transform into anything useful after the family gave up dinners for forty. Upstairs, the front and side bedrooms opened onto galleries around the courtyard. Thanks to Cousin Aylmer's father, most of the bedrooms, even the nursery, had adequate bathrooms. His money, too, had brought electricity and a semblance of central heating.

I had reached the doorway of the silent drawing room when someone came lightly across the hall, exclaimed "Petra," enfolded me in long arms and planted a kiss on one cheek. I drew back and found I was looking into the black eyes of another handsome man. The black hair was smooth, the skin tanned, the smile whimsical. It was all vaguely familiar. I frowned, then smiled; of course, it was the man who had asked the way in the lane.

"Petra," the voice said again and bent for another kiss. "I should have recognized you this afternoon," he whispered. "The light . . . but you didn't either." This must be Nico.

I turned the other cheek and found myself looking at our reflections in the wide mirror over the fireplace in the drawing room. Also reflected in the mirror was my nongamekeeper of the afternoon, now clad in evening clothes that turned him into a startlingly effective gentleman. He was taller and leaner than I remembered, his gray eyes intent as he watched us. A man who would be at home anywhere, I realized, and one who would stand no nonsense.

Nico and I separated and looked at each other. He was smoother than his brother and looked older, with, at least now, more conscious charm. He seized one hand. "Forgive me . . . I could not resist kissing you. It was spontaneous. Come have a drink with me. I still remember how we used to go exploring in the woods."

"I remember how she used to trip me up and then sit on my back and pull my hair," said a voice behind us. Amaury was on the bottom stair. "I wouldn't dare call her Peter now. She's changed." His glance was admiring, which made Nico look again.

"That was on your second visit, and I had to catch you off guard." I laughed as I glanced at the mirror. I did look well in the blue. Here was confirmation of what I knew, in London—that I had turned into an attractive person, even if I could never compete with Isabelle. Behind us the solid figure of the butler was pacing toward the East Indian temple gong under the stairs. Behind him came Eugenia, in her usual drab gray, trying to look composed.

"Oh, you're down." She beamed at the two men. "Come in. Manson will make cocktails, if you must have them."

"One of the triumphs of civilization is a perfect dry martini, someone once said," Nico remarked lightly and tucked my arm under his. Eugenia ignored this.

The white and gold drawing room was even more charming than I remembered, or perhaps I could appreciate it more now. Cousin Aylmer had seen that it was also comfortable, with armchairs by the couch and the formal chairs and love seat banished in groups around the room. I glimpsed the tall lean figure standing at the front windows and Eugenia's uneasy glance at it when Alexandra, handsome in off-white brocade, swept to a stance beside us.

"Oh, you're here, too." Eugenia contrived to look relieved and yet disapproving of the brocade. "Then I can introduce you all at once." The tall figure came to her side. "Lady Harborne, may I present Mr. Gavin Langlade. Pérdita, Mr. Langlade, my cousin Pérdita Norreys, and Nicholas and Amaury de Montluc." In an aside to Alexandra, she added, "Nicholas arrived after you had gone upstairs."

Mr. Langlade bowed to Alexandra, slightly less to me, and shook hands with the men.

"Gavin, you all know," Eugenia was continuing bravely, "is the new master of Aylforth Priory."

I should have known this afternoon. Now I smiled suitably, but I knew I was blushing beneath his impassive glance. Fortunately no one needed to say anything, for Alexandra took over.

"Nico, so glad you found your way. Mr. Langlade!" If she had had a lorgnette she would have raised it. "So you are going to take dear Aylmer's place?"

"No, Lady Harborne," he corrected easily. "No one could take his place. I am merely the next Langlade in line."

Her plump face softened. She had been fond of her brother. "If we had been informed at all"—she shot a hard glance at Eugenia, who looked away—"we might have been prepared for this sudden appearance. You must be James's great-grandson."

"And proud to be," he said softly. "I know the family

. . . . *21*

did not approve of his Scots bride. Yes, my great-grandfather was the younger brother of your grandfather.''

''Too bad none of our branch had sons—who lived,'' Alexandra said heavily, obviously thinking of Cousin Aylmer's children, dead with their mother in a resort fire before the war, and of her own boy missing at Dunkirk.

''Of course,'' the now pleasant voice was gentle. ''But, from my point of view, how fortunate I am to come into the family home.'' That was taking the bull by the horns, I thought, and saying out loud what all the county must be saying also. ''And to find such a charming new family.'' His glance, quickly veiled, was bland. ''I have never had a family, and I find the experience interesting.''

Alexandra's small hand patted the black-jacketed arm. ''I dare say you will do very well, Gavin. At least we hope so. And I, for one, welcome you.''

''Dear Cousin Alexandra.'' He bent from his height and brushed her cheek with his lips. ''You are the first to say that, and I thank you.''

''I am not surprised.'' She did not have to look at Eugenia. ''Come find me a martini.''

There was a bustle of sitting down around the couch, a passing of cocktails and some rather damp crackers. From my chair I could not help seeing Gavin as he straightened from speaking to Alexandra and how his gaze fixed on the doorway. It was Isabelle, I knew, late on purpose. Perhaps it was just as well if I could never really like this arrogant young man. All in soft pink tulle, Isabelle made an entrance, as always, and floated to a place on the couch sufficiently far from her mother. All three men hovered. I jerked my glance away and caught Alexandra's. Her left eyelid dropped in a slow wink. I grinned back, comforted. She and I had never been on winking terms before, though she had always been kind and amusing on her visits. And once she had told me that one stately blonde in a family was enough and that she herself had always preferred girls who were wiry and just five and a half feet tall and always into things. That had long been a solace.

"You look like an English rose, Isabelle," she said mellifluously. It was Cousin Eugenia who preened, her rather small eyes snapping with pleasure. Isabelle merely gave a demure smile. Then Roger Daintry arrived to make the table even, and there was talk of the roads and the weather and dinner was announced.

"Eight is always such a difficult number to seat properly," Eugenia complained, as she gestured to our chairs.

"You've been saying that for thirty years," Alexandra told her, "and you should know by now it never comes out properly." She moved without pause to Gavin's right as Isabelle went to his left. I found myself between Alexandra and Roger. The de Montluc boys, side by side opposite, looked at each other with cordial smiles.

"Now, Gavin"—Alexandra's voice took over the table as the soup plates were removed—"you must tell us more. Can you afford to keep up the place?"

"Alexandra!" Eugenia jerked her head agitatedly toward Manson, carving the roast at the sideboard.

"Don't be stuffy, Eugenia. Everyone knows everything in this house and village, anyway. Can you, Gavin?"

"I trust so, dear cousin." The broken eyebrow went up at a slant, and the firm mouth looked both relaxed and amused. I could not help resenting him, sitting there at the head of the table. Some people would judge his face interesting, I allowed, but the Montlucs were more handsome, and Roger, with his tan, had more of an outdoor look such as we admire in England.

"How? None of the family have ever had money since Grandpapa spent so much on the house and then more on fast women and slow horses. We know James, your great-grandfather, had none. What did your grandfather and father do?"

"Grandfather went to Canada and became a surveyor, Cousin Alexandra. My father turned engineer, and I am in the same profession. Manson is waiting, Cousin. Do you prefer your beef rare or well done?"

That shut her up for a while. As we waited for the vegetables, Gavin himself took over.

"It is a pleasure to have so many new cousins here." He sat back in the carved armchair and smiled around the table. "But I confess to bewilderment as to who is who. After all, our families never kept in touch, you remember. I have only been here for three very busy weeks, and there has been no occasion to discuss relations. I would appreciate a little genealogy. Cousin Alexandra, you and Cousin Eugenia were Cousin Aylmer's sisters?"

The brocade bosom beside me settled back. This was the sort of thing Alexandra loved. Three rings flashed white and blue lights as she toyed with the stem of the wine glass. "In-law," she corrected cheerfully. "Aylmer and I and dear Dick, who died in India, and Edward were brothers and sister. Eugenia is the widow of Edward, and Isabelle's mother."

"Gavin and Isabelle are third cousins," thrust in Eugenia from the foot of the table.

Alexandra ignored that. "Petra is also a cousin, though more distant."

"Perdita—that means lost." Nico halted the catalog. "Are you lost, Petra?"

"Oh, I have been ever since I left Aylforth," I answered, lightly amused, to turn aside a question I did not like. Perhaps I had been, once, but it was none of his business. I did not look at the man who had asked the same question earlier.

"Why Petra?" asked the head of the table politely.

"Pérdita was too much of a mouthful for her. First she called herself Dita; after a year or two she wanted to be called Peter. No one would, and she had to compromise," Eugenia explained flatly.

"And the gentlemen?" prompted Gavin.

Alexandra beamed at the Montlucs. I had always heard she had a weakness for handsome men. "A beautiful sister of my grandfather married a French count. Her grandson married a beautiful Hungarian princess who escaped with her two boys at the time of the fall of France. Aylmer welcomed them here for as long as they could stay. Roger, as you know, is our neighbor; the Daintry lands have marched with ours for generations."

Gavin bowed a little. "You have been most helpful, Cousin, but I know I will never learn the degrees of relationship."

"There's a tree in the family Bible, but there's no need to learn them," Alexandra said airily. "Just call us all 'Cousin' and you can't miss. Or, better still, drop the word."

"And some of you have lived here for a long time?"

He must know, for he had found Eugenia and Isabelle

obviously thoroughly established when he arrived. He must be just fishing for more information.

"Only three." The gay brown eyes looked down the table toward Eugenia, who became self-conscious. "Eugenia came here with her baby after dear Edward's death in France in thirty-nine and has acted most efficiently as chatelaine for Aylmer ever since." Eugenia looked more startled than pleased at the compliment. "Aylmer took Perdita under his wing that winter, after her parents were killed in an accident, so she and Isabelle grew up in the Priory until they went off to school, and until Perdita moved to London."

The broken eyebrow rose as Gavin smiled at Isabelle. "Then you both must know the house thoroughly."

Isabelle gave him her slow, beguiling half-smile. "I don't. I was never brave like Perdita. And I was too much younger anyway in those days for her to play with me—much."

She made it sound as if the gap between us was ten years rather than three.

There was a twitch at the firm mouth as Gavin cocked his head at me. "Then you're the one who knows all about the house?" There was no warmth in the question.

The only thing to do was to mock him. "Of course. Cousin Aylmer showed me all. I've numbered every stone for the American who comes along to buy the house." Both the Montlucs gave me wide-eyed glances.

"We will hope your knowledge will not need to be put to use." Coolly Gavin dropped the subject. I grinned at his annoyance and the slight shudder that ran around the table.

"Don't be unpleasant, Perdita," Eugenia said sharply,

in the tone she used to use so often when I was young. "There's no question of such a thing." But the question hung in the air after that, and out of the silence a mysterious remark came floating back to me.

"What is this about stolen pictures?" I asked brightly. "You mentioned them, Cousin Alexandra, when you arrived."

She brightened and leaned forward. "Yes. Most fascinating. You see . . . ."

"We will talk about that over coffee," Eugenia ordered loudly. Her sallow face flushed, and she pushed back a straying wisp of gray hair. "Come, Alexandra, girls, leave the men to their port."

She made for the door, but Alexandra got there first. I did not mind following Isabelle; I can enjoy something lovely even if I don't like it, and she had beautiful shoulders. At least her hair was still straight, though in a becoming French twist, and mine was as curly as when she used to envy it.

She remained standing in the drawing room, and when the men joined us, quite quickly, she adroitly cut out Gavin and strolled with him to the far windows, ostensibly to show him the view, though there was little to be seen in the dusk. Beside me, Roger dutifully called up memories of childhood exploits. The more he talked the more I recalled him as a nice, patient boy who was always Isabelle's slave. He hadn't changed, and in spite of his good manners his eyes followed her wistfully.

"Now, as to the pictures," began Alexandra when she had had three cups of coffee, the third in defiance of Eugenia's observation that she'd never sleep a wink after two. We all straightened at the words, and the two wanderers returned to nearby chairs. "The pictures probably have nothing to do with us at all."

"Of course they haven't." Eugenia took on a complacent look. "That's what I told some man who telephoned two weeks ago and asked if any of the Montluc pictures were here. He said he was calling from France, just to sound important, I'm sure. I cut him off quickly, and he sounded annoyed."

"But at least it is a good story." Alexandria ignored the interruption. "Nico, Amaury, it's your tale. Don't you want to tell it?"

The young men looked at each other questioningly. "You start, Amaury," Nico said easily. "I'll fill in, if necessary."

Amaury rubbed his cheek reflectively. "There isn't much to tell, or at least only what's been in the French papers. It goes back to our Montluc ancestors and their château at Montmézay near the Normandy coast. There were a lot of pictures, as always in these old places." He smiled deprecatingly. His English, as that of his brother, was faintly accented but impeccable. "Much of it was— is—worthless, oils and water colors by the ladies of the family over many years. But there were some good ones, too, and some whose values went up and down as tastes changed—Rigauds and Champaignes, for instance, but also Chardins and Watteaus, some of the Barbizon painters and some early Impressionists, bought perhaps with an eye to a bargain when the artists were young and struggling. A few were our mother's. I don't remember how many myself. Do you, Nico?"

The black head gave a shake, and the shoulders lifted. "We were too young. . . ."

"Quite. Anyway, when the war came we were staying at the château. Our father went to his regiment. Then the Germans were spreading out across Normandy. Thanks, I now know, to Cousin Aylmer and friends of our father who had plans ready, we escaped in a small boat to England. The Germans took over the château and soon began shipping pictures to Paris, where a great collection was being gathered at the Jeu de Paume to be sent to Germany. There Goering and Hitler's deputies would choose what they wished. The Germans began claiming some of our pictures were missing in spite of our leaving only with hand luggage.

"As you know, after the war the Allies appointed commissions to identify looted pictures and return them to their owners where possible. This has taken years. Just a month or so ago some of ours began to turn up, and the experts agree, according to an inventory our uncle had made, fortunately, in 1938, that pictures from Montmézay are indeed missing. Some may still be hidden in Germany; some might have been carried far away, others lost in the war . . . anything. The château has been searched, our uncle has asked neighbors, villagers. . . ." He spread his hands. "But nothing."

"Are the pictures so valuable?" asked Cousin Alexandra.

"Yes. Thanks to a copy of that inventory that was sent to New York with the idea of selling some furnishings some day, it is known what has vanished, some from the family collection, some bought by our mother and father —ten paintings altogether. Two Watteaus were Mother's; then there were a Chardin, Van Goghs, an early Manet, a Renoir, two Degases, and a small Monet.

. . . . *29*

Some would be our uncle's, the others would be ours, if found." He shrugged his shoulders. "The master list would straighten it all out. But that *if* is a big one."

"But why should anyone believe they are here?" Eugenia asked querulously.

"It is only the most remote of possibilities. It is just that when we escaped from France we came to Aylforth Priory, straight from Folkestone, and they might have been among the luggage."

"They weren't." Eugenia was very positive. "I was here when your mother and Maxim, that lame man she called her equerry, and you two boys were dumped on the doorstep. There were valises, but nothing as big as a crate and no pictures in the bags, either, for I helped unpack them."

I bet you did, I said to myself. You wanted to see what the Princess had saved. Then I realized she had left out Nanny. I almost started to remind her and stopped. Doubtless she had forgotten, and why mention Nanny now? On that distant day when the refugees had arrived I had been watching from my favorite hiding place under the rhododendrons below the terrace. I had lost my heart to the Princess, but I had hoped the plump, kind-faced Nanny would be looking after all the children.

"It is true we had only an hour when the news finally reached us of the waiting boat, after my father's command to flee," Amaury went on. "So," he shrugged, the first un-English gesture, "it is unlikely that we could have brought the pictures. But," he added proudly, "Mother did bring away her jewels. We are sure she sold them to help the Free French."

Nico's face went blank for a second, then he smiled deprecatingly at Gavin. "Since we are here to pay our respects to our kind cousin who helped us, we would like to look for the pictures. Even though it seems impossible, there is always a chance . . ." His voice trailed away.

"By all means," Gavin agreed pleasantly. "I'll tell Mr. Beckham, the estate manager, to show you around if you wish to search for places where pictures might be hidden." The subject was dismissed.

It was Nico who sat beside me next and began to talk of his school days and how he and Amaury had hated the place, and then after the war how they had gone back to the château. Then he and his brother had separated. Once I caught Isabelle watching us.

"But your mother—and your father?" I asked—tactlessly, I realized right away.

He had had long practice in not showing his feelings. "My father was killed in the first weeks, just after we escaped. My mother went to London to broadcast and work with the Free French. Toward the end of the war she went back to France and vanished."

I touched his arm. "I am so sorry," I murmured. "I remember your mother. She was beautiful."

"Yes, and gay and kind and good. That is how I remember her." He stopped; his voice changed and his glance was allowed to linger on me admiringly. "I should have recognized you this afternoon. I apologize again." He said it lightly. "You were unexpected . . . and I was confused. I was stupid to accept a ride with a friend and then lose the way. It's good of you not to betray me to the others."

. . . . *31*

"No one knew I was coming, and there is nothing to betray," I told him as lightly. But I remembered the voices in the wood. There had been nothing lost about whatever meeting had been in progress. However, it was not my business. Nothing really was my business here, any more, once the memorial service was over and I had done what I promised.

3

Yet, when I reached my room, in spite of the welcoming look of the bed, I went for a moment to sit on the window seat. That was another old ritual, whether I shared the room with Isabelle or Nanny, or, as later, slept alone. I always wanted to look at the trees and the park the last thing before sleep; sometimes I had even walked to bed with my eyes closed so as to hold intact the vision of the moon on the treetops and terrace. Then I would wait for Nanny to come and tuck me in and hear my prayers. She was my bulwark and my rock of Gibraltar, my mentor and a kindly grandmother. She never tried to be a mother; she had too much sense and principle for that. She never stepped out of her chosen role, but once, when I was sick, in a soft moment, she had whispered I was the tree on which grew the fruit of her heart. I did not understand, but I cherished the whispered phrase. When I was rebellious and tempestuous in my tomboy years she kept me out of the way of Eugenia lest she complain too often to Cousin Aylmer.

For I must have been a difficult child. Losing my home

and beloved parents, and not quite understanding my loss, I had felt abandoned when I first came, betrayed, and hostile to the Priory. Through my pores I gathered Eugenia's dislike and resentment at my intrusion into her domain. Cousin Aylmer and the housekeeper and maids had done their best for the orphan, but I distrusted all but Aylmer, who was a busy man. So I had escaped to the outdoors, wandering forlornly around the estate, playing my own game in which Mother and Father would drive up to the house in their fine new car for their darling daughter and whisk me away to where we three would be happy ever after. Even when I did realize my loss was permanent, that lost dream stayed in the back of my mind for years.

Cousin Aylmer understood because of his own desolation at the loss of his wife and small sons, from which he never recovered. One rainy day when he found me hiding in his closet he had taken me into his study and told me to read anything on the shelves. Suspicious at first, I had started with anything with pictures. Then, one evening, he had read me "The Cat Who Walked by Herself" and from then on I was a devotee of the written word and could work myself into any role I discovered. Here, through the coming years, was my real escape from the world Eugenia tried to impose around me.

First, of course, I was the cat, going my lone way and wishing I had a tail to wave. Then I was Mowgli and climbed nearly every tree on the place, though a fall and a broken arm did discourage me from trying to swing from branch to branch like the banderlog. The Western period, when I was both horse and the Black Rider, had mercifully been brief—there were very few Westerns on the shelves. But then I fell on Sherlock Holmes, Raffles and the Saint, and they were my admired and trusted friends for years. I soon took to making up my own tales, where I accompanied one or the other on a nocturnal exploit. Sometimes two or three times a week, I slipped around the Priory in quest of the stolen jewels or the wily murderer. With the Saint, my favorite as the most active and most debonair, beside me, how could I be afraid of even the blackest shadows? Occasionally I ventured out on the grounds. This took more courage, but sometimes a tale could only be carried forward outside the confines of the house. There had been the heroes of Scott and Dumas, too, Rider Haggard and Buchan, and, for a change in reading, the whole shelf of plays from Shakespeare to Shaw. Cousin Aylmer, so quiet and remote except for his constant duties to the estate, must have taken out a secret love of action and gaiety in his reading.

He had understood more than I had expected. One afternoon I ran away from some now-forgotten governess and climbed to the roof. For my own satisfaction I wanted to see if I could go all around the roof without having to come in a window. I thought Cousin Aylmer safely away, but he came home early and spotted my thin childish figure edging along from the roof of the back attic down to the ridgepole of the roof of the stables. He was waiting for me by the lattice on the last wall, and we went hand in hand to his study. I had no idea what was coming next—bread and water for days, I was sure. When we were facing each other in deep chairs he complimented me on walking the ridgepole and asked where else I had been. I never told him anything but the truth, so I hesitantly described my airy journey, suddenly conscious of the smuts and dirt I had gathered on the way.

He nodded gravely and filled his pipe. "I used to do the same thing, Perdita. There's a special feeling up there, above everyone, alone . . . you can see so far. . . ." He spent some minutes on his pipe. "I wish I could follow you still. I must have been a year older when I began my climbing days." He seemed almost proud of me. I was amazed and wished I might go sit on his lap as I had been permitted to do those first months. "Hmmm," he went on, "bare feet. You must have cut them. Well, I won't tell you not to do it again; you'll stop of your own accord in time. I watched you; you're agile and sure-footed. But I make one rule. Never go out on the roofs without rubber-soled shoes of some kind. I'll tell Nanny you must always have a pair. I won't even advise you to be careful because I know you have enough common sense not to try anything really dangerous. We won't tell anyone—this is our secret—but don't let your Cousin Eugenia catch you."

So, for several months, in rubber-soled shoes, I roamed at will. When I knew the roof well, the adventure was gone, and I stopped. But during that time Cousin Aylmer would ask me occasionally, solemnly, if I had had a good walk, and then wink. Something else which endeared him to me.

Dear Cousin Aylmer. He had been such a nice man, gentle, forgetful, but kind and fair and amusedly interested in my reading or other occupations when he had time from his duties. He had taken on burdens of tenants, villagers, neighbors; no wonder the whole county loved and respected him. The affection between us had grown steadily; now I wished I had seen him more these later years. It couldn't have been easy to take in a very small, very distant cousin, with Eugenia and Isabelle already ensconced; but there was no other relative with a large enough house, including Alexandra, I heard later, and he had never hesitated. The coming of Nanny must have been a boon to him.

Darling Nanny. It was she who had taught me to laugh at myself. Oh, not directly, usually, but by precepts and sayings about people getting too big for their britches, or guinea hens acting like peacocks, or just by laughing at my pretensions. When she laughed I had to join her, and so I learned. She showed me how to stand on my own two feet, also, and made me acknowledge when I was wrong and take the consequences, though sometimes she could soften the strong hand of justice; and she taught me to expect favors of no one except Cousin Aylmer. During those early years in London, when I was first trying to earn my own living, I'd blessed her and her teachings, and by the time they had faded a little the attitudes were firmly embedded. I'd gone my own way, these past seven years, and it had worked very well, thank you.

The loss of the Montlucs had been my gain, for after two or three months they went with their mother and the lame man to London and Nanny stayed behind. Three years later the boys had come back for the summer vacation. Eugenia had not resented them, and there was Nanny to look out for us all. Isabelle had tagged along once in a while, but usually she did not care for our games, since she was younger. Other times she and I had often played together amicably in spite of the difference in our ages, and had as often quarreled and gone our separate ways, though we shared Nanny and whatever governess was available. The war years, by and large, were blurs of memory except for pictures of helping in the gardens, orchards and kitchen and then escaping to the woods or a book.

I heard the front door open, and a figure, hands in pockets, strolled down the steps to the terrace toward the drive. From the height I was sure it was the new head of the house. I felt another spasm of dislike. In spite of his air of courtesy I was sure he had been mocking us all. How he must enjoy lording it here where his great-grandfather had been turned out because he had married an unknown Scots girl he had met in London. When later it was discovered her family was a good Highland one, though impoverished, the quarrel was too bitter to heal. And now her descendant was here as master! I could come to dislike this Gavin if he put on airs, though in fairness I had to admit he had not yet, really.

Inevitably I fell to wondering about him. He had been perfectly polite during the evening, but I had felt him withdrawn for some reason. Perhaps he did not trust us, although—or because—we were cousins! An engineer, he had said, in Canada. That would be why he had an easy way of walking, that deep tan, and eyes that looked as if they could see far as well as near. What kind of an engineer? His work must have taken him to wilds I could not imagine. He had not been at all put out by Alexandra's question about keeping up the place, and his clothes were right. Perhaps the surveyor grandfather

Return to Aylforth 38

had picked up the right pieces of land. If so, I could be glad for the sake of the estate. If Isabelle trapped him, and third cousins are quite far removed, they would make a handsome pair and I could wish her well. I'd be leaving soon, anyway.

Much as I loved Aylforth, and moved as I was to be here again, once my errands for Nanny were done, there was really nothing to keep me. I would perhaps drive into Devon for the pleasure it would give me and for a few days alone to think about what I would do next. But London was my life now. Somewhere I had once read that if you stood up to London and looked it in the eye, it would become yours. It had taken me a while. There had been those dreary days when I lived in a hostel and clerked at Woolworth's, having been turned down by Lyons because I looked too slender to carry trays. I had developed a deep hatred for our monetary system at Woolworth's, and this had driven me to a night course in stenography and typing. By sheer will power I had made myself a good secretary, and then I found London *could* be mine, for good secretaries with some intelligence were always scarce. Sure I could order my life as I wished then, I moved from my tiny flat to a larger one in the mews that was home now. If I had not driven myself so hard that I found myself suddenly exhausted, I might not have thought so soon of Nanny and Aylforth; and then the notice in the paper settled my mind.

Granted there was no one person drawing me back to the city, though I wished there were. The men I first met in the offices had bored me. Then I had learned my lesson, as Nanny would say. The whole first half year of my first success had held an added glow because I was happily in love with Ted. He was one of those blond, devastatingly handsome young Englishmen; and he was a good actor, too. We went everywhere together and were made much of. And we had such good times. I was inexperienced when it came to debonair young men, and of course I thought he intended marriage. Then, one Sunday evening, he told me excitedly of the fabulous offer to star in a new play in New York. A whole fresh world seemed to open for me. I had jumped up. "When do we go? I'll need a week to get new clothes before we are married." He had laughed lightly. "You *do* take things for granted, don't you, sweet. You're a big girl now, though. You should realize there's no *we* involved. We've had terrific fun together, and being seen around with you helped me, of course. But I'm on my way up, now, and no wife, charming as you are, is needed." I'd shown him the door and managed, I believed, to hide my black devastation, but I could still hear his delightful voice as I put my face in my hands for the hundredth time.

So I had never let myself be caught again, and that made it easier to enjoy the company of men and not be emotionally involved to the slightest degree. Of course I told myself that someday some man would be different, but there had been no sign of him yet. Perhaps I hoped for too much, but there was no hurry. In the meantime, I enjoyed my life, and that was more than many could say. And I was enjoying Aylforth, I had to admit, in spite of memories and problems. But soon I would have had enough of both.

If it had not been for Susan who brought me a plate of buns while I dressed, I would have had only tea to sustain me for the memorial service. Eugenia still ruled at breakfast; anyone not in the dining room on time had none—except Alexandra, who always had her own tray upstairs. I was grateful to Susan, for I felt lowly (a Nanny word) and it would have been worse without the buns.

All the ladies of the house wore decorous black. I annoyed Eugenia because I had brought a proper dress and went in my own car. As long as I had come, her attitude showed, I should parade with the family, but I was not sure how much I could take, either of the service or the mournful greetings afterward. So I parked alone at the edge of the meadow beyond the footpath and made my way among groups of people to the gray Norman church, built before the Langlades came, that held so many of their bones. A few of the villagers recognized me, and Mrs. Whalley of the sweets shop sent me a warm quick smile. I'd go to see her later. She must have put on two stone since I saw her last.

The family pew was full when I reached it, and it was Amaury who moved to the one behind so I might have a place. I did not glance at the others. The church was full, the county in the center; villagers, farm people, tenants, and townspeople from Shaftesbury and Salisbury crowded the small transepts and stood at back. When the organ began its familiar wheeze I gripped my prayer book and tried to empty my mind. I must not cry here and now. Cousin Aylmer would not care for that. It was the kind of service he would have approved: the right Bible selections, two of his favorite hymns, a moving tribute from Lord Hunston, the lord lieutenant, an old friend, and a good prayer where the vicar spoke quite firmly to God about the virtues of the departed and the good treatment he deserved in the hereafter. I sat straighter. It was all true, and I hoped Cousin Aylmer would be happy there.

When it was over, I stood aside for Cousin Alexandra to precede me up the aisle. She reached out and gave my arm a little squeeze. Cousin Eugenia and Isabelle passed without seeing me. As I turned to follow, a figure stepped back and I looked up into the impassive face of Gavin Langlade. There were tears in my eyes, which made me furious at myself, and I had to blink again before I could face the rows of anonymous faces. I wanted to run to the car, but I had to wait for the stately progress of those in front and the gentle handclasp of the healthily pink-faced vicar, Mr. Dormer. I skirted the group gathering around the cousins and the larger group beyond watching the gentry and made for my car. I could get back and change and perhaps disappear into the woods until dinner. I did not feel like talking to anyone.

I took back lanes to the Priory. The day was warm and cloudy, the leaves motionless. I wished it would storm, for when it cleared the weight of depression that surrounded me might lift. I felt I hadn't the strength to lift it unaided. The lanes from the home farm led me to the stableyard. I thought I saw a black car around the farther bend as I turned, but I might have been wrong. None of the other cars had yet returned. I went in by the hall door, started for my room, then turned to Cousin Aylmer's study. It was there I went to find him each time I came back to the house. I would go once more and say farewell to his shade.

Coming from the rear courtyard, the study was the

first room on the corridor. I pushed wide the half-open door. A strange man was standing by the window holding something flat. He was as startled as I, and for a second we stared at each other. Then something came down on the back of my head.

When I opened my eyes I was lying on the floor, not by the door of the study but beside the huge walnut desk. The colors of the Kandahar rug beneath me were muted by the gray light from the window. My head ached abominably. I pushed myself to my hands and knees and the room whirled. I waited a moment, reached up to the edge of the desk and pulled myself up until I could place both hands flat on the surface and steady myself against the tilt of the room.

"Looking for something on the desk, Petra? Or are you just trespassing again?" asked a cool voice from the doorway. "It seems to be a habit."

If I had tried to move I would have fallen. "Not trespassing," I croaked. "Cousin Aylmer's study. Always came here first." The room would have to settle in place some time.

"It is my study now." The voice had an implacable note. "You had a reason for coming here."

I started to shake my head and stopped quickly. "There was a man," I managed, " . . . by the window. There must have been another. He hit me." I could not look up.

"You're making this up. Eugenia once said you were fanciful; I can see why. There is no one in the house, for I have been through it looking for Manson. I'd have seen anyone leaving. Come, now, what is it you're after?"

One hand moved slowly to the top of my head. "He hit me," I repeated stupidly. "There's a bump."

"There has been no one here to hit you." He was exaggeratedly patient. "Are you looking for another treasure?"

"Must have been two men," I repeated painfully. I remembered something else. "A black car . . . at the turn of the lane."

"No car was there when I passed. We'll not mention this . . . incident. Hadn't you better get ready for luncheon? It will be ready soon."

"They had time to leave before you came." I was stubborn about it. "And I don't want any luncheon." The thought nauseated me. I knew I sounded childish and I was annoyed with myself for not coping better, but I was still dizzy. I started to turn and felt myself swaying. Firm hands came from behind and caught my elbows, held me upright, then dropped. The room shifted again. I put out a hand to steady myself somehow and it landed on an arm as solid as steel. I waited, willing myself to stay erect, took a step to the open door, wavered and clung to the arm. At the third step the door was safely in place and at the fourth the arm fell away. I could not help looking up at the man beside me.

The face, the gray eyes, were intent and watchful, with a shadow of a smile behind them. "You're putting on quite a good act; I am forced to admire it." I took another step. "Your bag. You dropped it—somehow." The handle was thrust over my hand. I made it to the door, rested a moment. "I'll tell them you are lunching in your room." I wanted to answer but nothing came.

As I crept up to my room, fortunately meeting no one,

I was dizzy from surprise and shock as well as the blow. Who had hit me on the head, and why? It seemed senseless. There had been someone else beside the unknown man by the window. Unexpected and causeless violence was frightening. But my head hurt too much to try to think. My last thought, after I took two aspirins and subsided on my bed, was that I should have made Gavin feel the bump—then he might have believed me.

It was past teatime when I awoke, ravenously hungry and with a sore place on the top of my head but no headache. As far as I could tell, peering over my shoulder in the bathroom mirror that was now too low, the skin wasn't broken, and the short curls hid the bump. It could not have been a very hard blow, fortunately. I hurried into a sweater and skirt and went down the second floor corridor to the backstairs to the kitchen.

Mrs. Mellowfield welcomed me with open arms. "Miss Petra! I was wondering when you'd seek me out. You'll be wanting tea, as usual. Sit down at the table and you'll have it. The water's on, for I was making my own."

She was grayer than I remembered, and she had lost some weight, but had kept enough for a comfortable figure. Her brown eyes and pink cheeks were as bright as ever. As I watched her bustle to the stove, I began to take in the new glories around the room. The kitchen was painted white, now, with a huge new white stove where the old coal stove had sat so long, and white cupboards lining the walls. It could never be truly modern, but it certainly was an improvement.

"It's good to see you, Petra." We were old friends. She set two pottery cups before us, a loaf of fresh bread, a crock of new butter and one of damson jam and drew up a chair. "But it's a sad, sad day for us all." She shook her head, and I knew I could not let her dwell on the sadness too long.

"And it's good to see you, Mrs. Mellowfield. I should have come to say hello last evening."

"Dead tired, I heard you were, so I did not expect it. See, now, how Mr. Aylmer himself fixed up my kitchen for me last year, and my room upstairs, too? Said he got a bit ahead in his funds and could think of no better way to spend it. Mrs. Langlade herself couldn't get me to leave."

She and Cousin Eugenia had skirmished half-heartedly for years.

"Tell me, though." I sipped the strong tea greedily. "What was the matter with Cousin Aylmer? I only saw the notice in the paper by chance five days later."

Her round face beneath the neat braids looked shocked. "And did no one write you? No, they wouldn't. A heart attack it was; he went in his sleep. Dr. Calstock knew he had trouble these last years and might go any time. Mr. Aylmer wouldn't let him tell anyone. It do seem longer than a month."

A month ago. That was when I was working night and day. I'd picked up a paper I hadn't read so as to rest a few minutes and there had been a short nice piece about him. I'd grieved for an unhappy day and put it all behind me, but I had watched for the notice of the memorial service that was to be announced later.

"Mr. Thetwin, the solicitor in Salisbury, you know, already knew about Mr. Gavin, though, and he came quickly," Mrs. Mellowfield went on. "And I'm sure we are fortunate in him. But a kinder man than Mr. Aylmer never drew breath." Her round chin began to tremble. We looked at each other and then quickly out of the window at the walled garden.

"But Mr. Gavin, now," she went on firmly, "he'll do. Unaccustomed he is, of course, to our ways, but he listens—to all of us. He's come and asked me for tea here several times and sits and chats just as you do. He's used to working with men, I hear, and all ours respect him. And businesslike! Mr. Beckham says he'll have the place making money yet."

At the moment I didn't want to hear anything good of Mr. Gavin. I thanked her for the tea and said I'd be back for a good talk, but now I wanted some air before dinner, and I was gone from under her eyes as quickly as in the old days. I circled the box hedge, decided I did not really feel like walking, and started down the yew alley to the silly white summerhouse at the end. I could sit there in peace for half an hour and gird up my spirits for dinner.

Five minutes had gone and the girding was not very successful, though the sun was helpfully trying to break through the clouds in the west, when Roger Daintry found me. Thus it was Roger who first questioned me. He opened awkwardly by saying he'd seen me walking in the alley, which was possible, and just wanted a chat. Hadn't seen me for years, with which I could cordially agree. With that topic exhausted, he got up and strolled around the statue of a nymph, poised, like Horatius in his harness, on one knee. The contrast with the solid, tweed-clad figure was delightful.

He sat down and tried again. "Tell me, Petra, don't

you remember anything at all about the Montlucs arriving and all their luggage?"

"Not really." I leaned back against the hard marble back of the bench that ran around the pavilion. "Why do you ask?"

He flushed, his expression both dogged and miserable. "Isabelle told me to because Nico told her to find out, twice. She's so kind, she always likes to help people."

That wasn't my picture of Isabelle, but I knew he believed it. I eased to my feet. "You can tell her I don't remember a thing about the luggage." Which was perfectly true. "If you're coming to dinner you better go and change."

"You're right. She doesn't like me to be late. I'll tell her what you say and she'll be glad to tell Nico."

That required no comment.

At dinner, during the roast, Cousin Eugenia, who until then had not shown she knew I was present, suddenly stared in my direction and raised her voice. "Are you leaving before lunch tomorrow or after, Petra? I must know about the order."

In spite of myself I looked at Gavin and was pleased to see his gray eyes widen in surprise. I glanced at the other end of the table. "I hadn't given it a thought, Cousin Eugenia," I told her quietly.

"But surely . . ." she began, when Gavin cut in smoothly.

"There's no thought of Petra going tomorrow."

"Certainly not." Cousin Alexandra's round voice dominated all. "She had a long drive here and she must still be tired. She needs a few days of a good rest and feeding.''

"No one is being asked to leave." Pleasant as his voice was it carried an authority that could not be questioned. "In fact, I hope all my cousins will stay until we can get to know each other, investigate the matter of the pictures further—until your own affairs call you away. Or until other arrangements are made here.''

We were both looking at Eugenia. Her mouth actually fell open, and her expression shifted from malice to comprehension to anger. I was sure she had never thought but that she and Isabelle would go on living at the Priory while she managed the house and enjoyed her status with Gavin as she had for so many years with Aylmer. Gavin's expression did not change from bland kindness as he glanced at us all.

The Montlucs bowed and murmured and Cousin Alexandra agreed. "Good of you, my dear Gavin, and quite proper. Of course we'll all be glad to stay on. Now I'm here I certainly have no intention of picking up and leaving immediately.''

The others began to talk to cover the vanquishing of Eugenia. Warmed by Gavin's quick reply on my behalf, I leaned back a little and surveyed the table. It was like a stage set, a social comedy of course, built around a group of handsome, smiling people. But would there be sufficient complication for a play to work itself out? I doubted it. After all, we were cousins, tenuous as that bond usually is. But they were fun to watch. And it was good to have a family again.

I must have smiled, for Alexandra grinned at me. I hoped I would get to know Cousin Alexandra better.

There was no chance that evening. Plied with good advice about a hot-water bottle and the comforts of warm milk on retiring, she literally shooed me upstairs even before the coffee. I was glad to go. Let the past come back if it would. And my head was aching again. From the foot of the stairs I saw Gavin lead Isabelle to that love seat while the other three men watched.

4

But what persisted in poking up in my mind when I snuggled on the window seat that night was not the first time I saw Nanny, but my last visit with her.

It had been last September. My first pleasant success was behind me, and I was about to settle down to my hoped-for second. The letter that came was in her careful round hand, which mine still resembled, for she had first taught me to write. The note was short. She was not feeling quite herself, and it had come to her that she would like to see me again. There was no one at the Priory, for they were all off shooting, I realized. I could come any time and she would be glad to see me. It was signed "Love." I knew that she must be ill if she said she was not feeling herself, for she was always given to understatement. I took the morning train the next day and the local taxi from the station.

The house was very quiet as I stalked upstairs. Now midafternoon, the servants would be asleep or down at the village. From habit, I turned to the nursery and put down my bag and heard her calling, "Petra? Is that you?"

Next door, down the side corridor, she was in her own bed, her white hair in two neat braids tied with blue ribbon, wearing one of her white cotton nightgowns with ruffles at the collar and wrists. The high color was gone from her cheeks, and her blue eyes looked paler and a little anxious. She held out her arms and we hugged each other and she smelled of lemon verbena soap as always.

"I knew you'd come," she said contentedly but a little breathlessly as she leaned back against the stack of pillows. "You were always the one I could trust. It was silly, but in my mind I called you Douglas sometimes—you know, the poem."

I nodded. I hadn't deserved that, for I had plagued her enough, and I managed to say so. She was smaller there in the bed, and shrunken. She gave a ghost of a chuckle. "You were no trouble, really, Petra, for you always were honest and truthful. Mischievous, yes, but I'd rather have that than Isabelle's sneaking ways and downright lies. Not but what her mother was much to blame for them, the way she ruled the girl." She patted my hand. "You were a nice child, Petra, and I hope you still remember to say your prayers and brush your teeth."

I put my hand over hers. "Yes, Nanny, I do. But what can I do for you? Isn't there anything you want?"

"Want? Oh, no, thank you. Mrs. Mellowfield does very nicely and takes good care of me. Mr. Aylmer told her to, you know, but she would, anyway. Totten, too; but he's getting a trifle old for his duties, though I always thought a butler's life was the easiest below stairs. But we aren't getting any younger, are we? You look well, and that's a nice suit—tweed's always good. You can take care of yourself now?''

"Yes, and you, too, if you'd let me." Remorse that I had not come to see her more often was washing around me.

"Oh, there's nothing needed like that, dear. I wouldn't want to leave my own room, you know, and the Priory's home. But I did want to tell you about my will.''

"Will? Don't talk of such things, Nanny.''

"Oh, yes, dear. There's a time for everything, and a will's one of them. I could wish there was more for you, but there's some money in the bank and something will be left over after I'm buried. And there's my trunk, if you can use anything.''

"Trunk?'' I tried to envision her with one.

"You might not remember. That big old valise was all I had when I came, but my sister sent down clothes from Scotland and I knew there'd be things I would want to put away. Then the Princess left a few of her clothes for me to keep for her and my room wasn't the proper place. So I found this great high square trunk, empty, too, in the attic, not at all the kind anyone would want any more. I asked Mr. Aylmer if I could use it. He went up with me, pulled it out in the light and said if it was what I needed it was mine. He even went up with black paint and put my initials on the top and the side so there'd be no mistake, ever.''

She smiled at the memory. I could see the attic under the low eaves and the soft dust on the floor and Cousin Aylmer drawing the initials as carefully as if he were filling in a map.

"So I just put the valise inside and everything of mine in on top of it. There are some old clothes I'm ashamed of now, Petra, that I never got to throw away, and some I thought I'd fix and never did. I'm not up to the clearing out, but you throw them away; they'd be no use to anyone. But the new bathrobe the Princess gave me is there; I never could bear to wear it for it made me think of her. It might be a mite large, but it will keep you warm winters.''

''New bathrobe?'' I asked automatically—something else I had not remembered.

''You'd not have seen it, for I kept it in the valise. She put it in for me and even the three pictures from my room I'd grown fond of, and she said I could have them when I asked. Only an hour we had to pack, with the English boat coming to take us away. The Princess said she'd do the bags if I'd take the boys to the kitchen and keep them quiet and fill up a picnic basket with all the food I could find. No knowing how long we'd be on the way and the boys were always wanting something to eat. It was lucky I found a big basket, too, for we had to hide along the coast a bit and then make a run for it, they said, and hide again. But the Princess got all the bags packed all by herself. I remember I was sorry she used the old leather ones and not the new pretty ones, but she was right, what with the rain and salt spray. She and Maxim, the one she called her equerry, who had come with her from her home, they carried them down to the shore, and the boys and I carried the basket.''

''It must have been scary, going off in the night like that.'' She was enjoying the remembering.

''I didn't like running away, but I knew it was sensible. I didn't want to be around Germans. Everything was planned. But some horrid men were waiting on the shore; someone must have told them we were leaving. They hadn't dared come to the château. Made us open the bags and put their nasty hands in them. One had my shift and corsets right on top. That made them laugh and they didn't look any more. If I hadn't had to hold the boys, I'd have told those men what I thought of them. As it was, Amaury flew into a rage. He always had a wicked temper, you remember, used to bully his older brother when he thought I wasn't noticing. There was no one he loved so much as his mother, and he knew the men were trying to bother her, you see. But I held him and the English boat came then and it was all right, for the men just went away." She stopped and closed her eyes.

"Shall I get our tea?" I asked, and she nodded with a ghost of a "Please."

Mrs. Mellowfield had embraced me, shaken her head dolefully, and thrust a tray into my hands.

"Always a nice tray Mrs. Mellowfield sets," Nanny said approvingly. "She and I have been good friends these many years. I've given her what I wish her to have, and I've sent things to my niece at Fort William and my cousin at Greenock. At first I thought I'd take the things to the people in the village myself, but that's not the proper way, and I couldn't bear the way they'd talk to try to cheer me. So it's all written out for you, the names and the gifts. Promise me now you'll take them around yourself."

I took her hand in both of mine. "I promise." The shadows were beginning to rise in the corners of the room.

"Then I know you will." She sighed. "There's no hurry, mind. Just come sometime when you can and take care of it all. And the will, now. There's a copy in the trunk and the real one is with Mr. Thetwin, in Salisbury —all proper and legal and waiting. He has the key, too. He'll see to the burying, but the rest is for you to do.''

She dozed then, and I must have also, for next Mrs. Mellowfield was bringing up supper for the three of us. She and I talked of old days, and Nanny's eyes brightened and she laughed almost like herself. I was cheered when I left her for the night.

We had breakfast together the next morning, porridge and kippers and strong tea such as London does not know. She ate a bit of everything and said there was nothing like company to give a body an appetite and told me my hair was untidy and she hoped I read the Bible every day. ''Ruffled your hair is,'' she added unexpectedly, ''like the Princess', daytimes.''

''But the face beneath is different.'' I smiled. ''I remember how beautiful she was.''

''She was that, but you do very well in spite of your freckles, and your eyes don't look too big for your face any more. Handsome is as handsome does, I'll thank you to remember, miss.'' She was quite lively. ''The Princess was a lovely lady, though. I never knew a better. Pity neither of the boys took after her. I was sorry not to keep them, but she wanted them in London in school, where she could keep an eye on them. I always was sure they needed a strong hand.''

''Which you'd have given them, and sometimes on their rears.''

''And where does it do more good, I ask you? Though Nico needed it less; he'd go his own way, but he could be led, too. She said they were doing nicely in school.''

"When was that?"

"Why, the last summer of the war. Just after all our soldiers went to France. Three times she was at the Priory: the summer after we came, then when she had a spell of the flu and needed a rest and more than she got—the boys came without her once—and then the last time when you were all away visiting and Mr. Aylmer was out with the home guard. She was that disappointed. Said she wanted to thank him for all he'd done for her, and more than anyone ever knew, I'll be bound, and to ask him for advice. She came right up here to the nursery, and we had tea. She didn't look well at all that day, thin and white and her curls flattened and her big eyes like burned holes in a blanket. I told her right out she wasn't eating and sleeping enough, but she just laughed and said she'd make all that up later.

"She asked if she could get a suit she'd left with me, since she had a bag. I told her it was in the trunk in the attic, so she went for it to save me the stairs, and I pressed it for her then and there, while she looked around the room and said the three pictures I'd brought from France looked at home here in the frames Jim— you remember the gardener's boy—made for me.

"All the time she was restless, though. She was going away for a bit and was I sure there wasn't any way to reach Mr. Aylmer. But there wasn't, for it was all secret and no one knew where he was. She wasn't happy in London now, though she liked to think she was doing her share for the French. Strange people were coming over from France, she said, and her own friends leaving and no one she knew well enough to trust except us and Maxim.

" 'You must have friends or lawyers or a bank, my lady.' I was trying to cheer her up.

" 'No.' She shook her head. 'And with the bombs—you never know what they'll hit next. I'm glad the boys are out in the country now.'

" 'There are no bombs here', I said. 'You came and stay a bit and get rested. Mr. Aylmer will take care of anything for you.'

"She jumped up then. 'Yes. He will. And the Priory is safe from bombs. I'll go and write him a note, and everything will be all right until I, or Maxim, come down again.'

"She went off to the study and came back and showed me the envelope. It just said, 'To be held until called for by me or my representative,' and her initials. I promised to give it to him when he came home. So she kissed me and said to give you her love and thank you for all the things you'd shown her about the Priory, which seemed a little odd, dear, but I didn't question, and by the time you came home I'd put it too far away in the back of my mind. The first evening Mr. Aylmer was home I put the note right on top of the papers on his desk, but he never spoke of it, and it wasn't my place to ask him, then, or when we heard she wouldn't be coming again, ever."

She must have had a good reason to be jumpy, I thought, since she had not returned from wherever she was going. Poor lady . . .

"So she said she had to get back to see her boys," Nanny was going on, "and left to walk to the station. So that was the last time I saw her, but I've always been glad we had that visit."

"I remember the boys," I said. "One with blond hair and one dark. We played in the woods."

"They were good boys," she murmured, "though head-strong. And Amaury had that temper they kept saying came from his great-grandfather, the French one, which was no excuse to tell a child. I hope the scar on Nicholas' shoulder healed. You remember Nicholas had laughed at him, and Amaury shoved him so hard he fell backward on the hoe the gardener's boy had left lying with the blade up. Ten stitches it took, but Nicholas wasn't angry; he never could be for more than five minutes."

"It served him right, though. He was jeering at Amaury because he was grieving over a dead bird."

"They were a handsome pair, but there's no telling what they'll turn into. But I could always be sure about you."

The bluish eyelids began to droop, and the fine lines deepened around her eyes. "Watch your time, child. You'll forget and miss the train." Her voice was lower. I leaned over and hugged her again and we kissed on both cheeks; we only kissed rarely, she and I, we didn't need to.

She sat up straight. "I'm glad you came, Petra. It's done me good to see you. Be a good girl, now, and come again when you can."

"I will, oh, darling Nanny, I will," I had promised. But I hadn't. New problems had come up in London. And four months later it was too late. Mrs. Mellowfield wrote me Nanny had died in her sleep, and Mr. Thetwin wrote that she had been buried at Mr. Aylmer's request beside the family plot and there was a small savings account for me and what was described as a tin trunk in an attic and would I be coming down to claim them. I sent a note that I couldn't manage just then and that I'd come when I could. And then, of course, I put it off. I was too busy, I told my conscience whenever it bothered me. Now I was here I could take care of Nanny's bequests and be on my way in a day or so. I had a little spasm of indignation that no one at Aylforth had yet asked what I'd been doing in London these past years, but I laughed myself out of that. There was no one here any more who would care.

Right after breakfast, and after making my bed, earning shy thanks from Susan, I went in to Nanny's room. Those three pictures she had brought from France. . . . I knew them by heart, a wildly overcolored woodland scene, a stark cottage and moors, no doubt to remind her of Scotland, and some cheerful Breton peasants dancing down a road. They were nothing, but might another picture have been framed with each one?

In the next room, where she had lived, the morning light showed the worn rug, coverlet, curtains. Nothing was changed, for there was no longer any need to use the room. It was too familiar. I went for a moment to the window that looked east toward the wide fields and the hills lifting beyond. She'd liked the view, though once she'd allowed that the one from her room in France had been better—more to see, she'd put it.

The back of each of the pictures was covered with stiff cardboard, and there was no space for another picture within the shallow frames. I had just hung the last one when Amaury came in.

"I was in our room and heard you leave the nursery,"

he said easily. "I've already looked at those pictures. Nothing there."

"It's my nurse's old room," I told him stiffly. "I've a perfect right to look at anything."

"Don't be prickly, Peter. She was my nurse first, remember? Come along for a walk. It's a good day." He was tall and broad, but not heavy, and had a certain vigorous grace. The light-blue eyes were laughing as he slipped an arm through mine. "Let's go and see if we can't remember something together."

It was indeed a lovely day, warm and just a bit misty. I did want to walk, preferably alone, but that appeared impossible. So I laughed back at him and we went along the corridor and down the stairs, arm in arm. The post had come, and Gavin was slipping it through his long fingers as he listened to Mr. Beckham, the estate manager, I remembered. Gavin lifted his head and nodded to us and went back to the letters. I heard him say in a decisive but easy voice, "It may be custom, but we'll do it my way this time, Mr. Beckham, and leave that field fallow and put drains in at the Williams farm next week."

"A dour character," remarked Amaury as we went down the steps from the parterre to the terrace.

"Dour and often unpleasant," I agreed.

"Oh, I don't know. A bit lordly, perhaps, but who wouldn't be—becoming lord and master of an estate like this overnight? And if you're an engineer you're used to being obeyed. And that Cousin Eugenia does need a setting down sometimes. Does her good. Where shall we go?"

He might well be good company on a long ramble

some time, but not now. "How about the village?" I suggested. "It's only a mile, and that's all I feel up to now."

"Righto. We'll find a pub. Haven't been in a real English pub since I was old enough to have a beer."

We set off down the drive. "Where have you been all these years?" I asked idly.

"We were in England almost seven years—briefly with a French family, then in some little school in London, then outside in the country nearby. I don't remember much, now, but Maman came to see us often. Cousin Aylmer must have helped her. We saw Cousin Alexandra once or twice, but then she went off to the States with her husband the General, on some war business. We had a bloody time of it for a while at school, I can tell you, but we never let Maman know how much we hated it; she had enough on her mind, we realized. A year or more after the war we went back to the château."

"Your mother . . . ? Nico just said she vanished. I must have put that out of my mind."

He broke a leaf off a rhododendron and began to tear at it with wide brown fingers. "Yes. We never could find out what happened. She had wanted to go to France all along, but they wouldn't let her until after the invasion. They probably thought it would be safe then. Nico and I didn't know. She told us she was going away for a short while to do what she could to help. She parachuted into Normandy, and someone may have recognized her, betrayed her. No one ever could learn what happened. And the next week Maxim was killed in a bombing raid on London."

"I'm sorry," was all I could manage.

He patted my arm. "Yes. Such a waste. I still miss her, even after all these years. I've always been glad I live at Montmézay; I seem closer there to her and father, though I know that's silly."

It was very touching, and I liked him the more for telling me. "You live at the château?" I couldn't just drop the subject.

"Of course." He sounded surprised. "It's my uncle's. My father was his second brother. Uncle came back after the war—he'd been a prisoner—and we're working the farms and trying to make them pay and running a small agricultural school to try to get young people to stay on the land instead of going to the big cities. It all eats up money. That's why he couldn't help hoping to find out about the pictures. He sent us over to London to see Cousin Alexandra . . . if she knew anything. He'd heard about Cousin Aylmer. Then there was this piece in the paper about the memorial service, so we all came down. I don't mind saying I'd like a share for myself so I can get my own place; I've an eye on one near enough to Uncle to help, yet I could be independent, too."

I glanced at his broad-shouldered figure. He was large for a Frenchman, perhaps due to the combination of English, Norman and Hungarian blood. It was evident he could cope with any work on a farm. His brother, now, was more the city type, slender and a bit under Amaury's six feet.

"The school's a blessing for Uncle." He tossed aside the shredded leaf and smiled down. "First he took in war orphans, naturally. He lost his only son, you see, in the first fighting and his son-in-law a week later, and his daughter died when the baby was born. When the supply

. . . . *63*

of war orphans became low he took up the school idea and had me take some agricultural courses so I could help. Now he almost puts me in the place of his own boy; we've been together so long, and there are only the two of us."

"Then Nico isn't with you?"

"Nico on a farm?" He threw back his head and hooted. "Never. He never took to country life, was stubborn about it, too. We must have different genes." He shrugged. "Finally he kicked up a row and Uncle sent him to some cousins in Marseilles in the wine-import business. But Nico couldn't stick that either. He went off to Algiers on his own. Wrote me he liked it, there were all sorts of things you could turn your hand to if you were clever. But he might have been too clever, for he sent me a scrawl saying he was in a spot of trouble and would have to change his name and go away for a while; but he'd come for a visit when it was cleared up and he had enough money. He was twenty when all that happened, and we never saw or heard from him for ten years until he turned up at the château a week or so ago."

"Didn't your uncle try to find out about him?"

"After a few months. But all he could learn was that Nico had set up a little business of his own and wasn't doing badly and then had gone about his passport to the consul and said he was going on a buying trip to India and Hong Kong. That was about the time he wrote me. After that—nothing."

I was thinking of a boy starting off for a place like Algiers at the age of twenty. But then I had done the same thing at eighteen, to sink or swim in London.

Obviously both of us had been able to swim, and I hoped his lessons had come more easily than mine.

"You must have had a lot of catching up to do when he came back."

"We talked every chance we had." Amaury grinned. "He wanted to hear about our childhood and our parents and our time in England to check all the things he'd thought about so much when he was so far away. Being in business and then fighting in Indochina must have taught him to keep quiet about himself. Says he's going to live in Paris now, no matter what. He'll marry a rich girl some day, with his looks."

There was no envy in his words, but as I glanced at him I thought there would be many who would think him more attractive than the wandering brother.

"Nico was always the smart one, too," Amaury went on cheerfully. "I had the strength, and I admit a temper, and he had the brains, but no one easier to get along with. He says I've changed, but I think he has too; tougher and wants his own way more, dead serious too. He did say he was ashamed of swiping father's signet ring when he went off so as to have something he could keep from the family, and was glad Uncle had given me his. But he's the same old Nico, just wants a good life in Paris."

"And you want a good life in the country," I pointed out.

He agreed instantly. "Right. But we both need enough money to live properly."

"Cousin Alexandra is obviously glad to see you."

"Wonderful, isn't she? Made me feel like family the minute I walked in, and Nico, too, when he came."

"You didn't cross together?"

"Oh, he had some business in London and went ahead, but he spent the night with us and said he had to see a man but could get a lift down to the Priory and meet us here. Silly of him to lose the way." The tone was affectionately indulgent. He halted as we came to the village. "I remember this, a little. It looks just the same. It's the sort of thing you think of when you think of 'England.'"

It was true. The small, small green, the church at one end and the inn at the other, the low cottages between—all was just as it had been twenty years before. The sweets shop had a fresh red trim around the bow windows and some of the thatched roofs were gone—that was all. Too small a place to attract new enterprise, I told myself thankfully. Constable Tompkins went by on his old blue bicycle, nodded solemnly and touched his cap. I hoped he'd recognized me. At The Oak and Ivy I wondered if Tim Carrick still owned the place, for the man behind the bar was a stranger, but I didn't ask.

Amaury almost pushed me to a table in the corner and came back with two beers. "Much better than French," he said approvingly after settling into the low armchair. "I'd forgotten . . . and how nice pubs are too, cozy and quiet."

"Not of an evening," I reminded. "This is probably a mass of beer drinkers and darts players then."

He grinned, took another quaff and propped his head on one hand, gazing at me intently. "Things English have been coming back to me ever since I landed. How about you, Petra? Of course you don't remember everything when you were small, but don't things come back to you, now you're here again?''

"Some do and some don't,'' I agreed absently.

"But now, big events would. I'm sure our arrival was a big event in your young life.'' He was half mocking, half serious. "I bet you were hidden somewhere and watched us.''

"How well you remember me,'' I mocked in turn. "Yes, I was, and I did.''

"I knew it. And it must have been in your mind this past day. There were bags, I remember that myself. Nico and I each had a very small one, for a toy or two, we'd gotten them ourselves. Mother had a heavy one, I know because I sat on it when we waited, in the dark on the shore in France and at Folkestone. Nanny had an old valise she wouldn't let us sit on. But bundles now, anything rolled up or flat and done up in paper? Do you recall anything like that being taken from the car?''

I shut my eyes to think, but could see nothing. A roll? That was possible; I might not have noticed. I opened my eyes to say so and found myself looking across at Gavin in the doorway. His gaze swept over the two of us and he turned to the bar. Annoyed at him and me and Amaury, I stuck out my tongue at his back, and only then realized there was a mirror behind the bar. Amaury had been looking at his beer. I put on a rapt expression. What had I been going to say, oh, yes, a bundle. "I can't say there wasn't a roll or a bundle,'' I began slowly. "There could have been, but with things piled up and people coming out from the house I might not have seen it. But I can't say definitely that there was—or wasn't.''

"But there *might* have been,'' he emphasized. "Mother

was practical and had a good mind under that mop of hair, they tell me. She must have known we wouldn't be back home soon. She might have wanted to provide for us somehow and not wished to touch the family funds in England, with the future so uncertain and all. But what did she do and how?" He was watching me and I was only conscious of the approaching figure.

"That was not a very ladylike thing to do," said the cool voice above us, "particularly in public. I'm surprised."

I had to look up. Were the gray eyes amused? I could not see in the dark room, but the aquiline face held no expression. Amaury started to rise. Gavin gestured. "I'd better run you back; it's nearly lunchtime and you will be late if you walk."

We had no chance to protest, for he paid for the beers and marched ahead of us and held open the door of the Land Rover. Amaury gave me a comic look and clambered in the back.

"Do you find the village very different from Scotland and Canada?" I cooed to the profile beside me. I wasn't going to let him think he could intimidate me all the time. I was still quite certain someone had hit me in the study, even if he wasn't.

"Very different from Canada," he answered as politely. "I am hardly an authority on Scotland and its villages."

"No need to be when you are on so many other things," I agreed and settled into silence, hoping he knew what I meant.

In the hall Amaury grabbed my hand. "It was good

talking with you, Petra. Look here, don't you know something about paintings?''

I shook my head. "No. And if those missing pictures were hanging on the walls, everyone would have known it long ago. You'll be looking for where they might be hidden, and there isn't a chance in a thousand they're here.''

"Yes. But come along on our search anyway. You might be a help. You don't know how we need you.''

I said I would because his eyes were anxious—more than they needed to be, I thought, and wondered why.

5

"What time are we all going to make a tour of the house?" demanded Cousin Alexandra as she unfolded her napkin.

"We?" Two thin lines appeared between Gavin's dark brows. "I thought it a matter for Amaury and Nico only."

"Oh, it is, any real search, that is. They'll probably turn the place inside out eventually," she agreed cheerfully. "But since Mr. Beckham is going to show them around the rooms, so to speak, I thought I'd like to go along for a bit. It's years since I've seen anything but the first floor and my own room."

"You won't find it changed much since you were a girl," Eugenia observed sourly.

"But it's so long ago we were young." Alexandra's voice was honeyed. "I'm sure I've forgotten a great deal. But of course you inspect everything every day. But Petra might like to come, anyway."

I nodded. I had agreed, but I could slip away soon. The thought of people prodding and prying was distasteful.

"I'm going to enjoy just looking around," said Amaury with real enthusiasm. "Mother loved it here."

I glanced at the two Montluc faces but I could see no signs of the Princess' piquant beauty. Perhaps the next generation would have it. How I had admired her! At first she had seemed like a fairy come from beneath one of the mounds to visit mortals for a while. I'd watched her whenever I could. When she came for the next visit I was eight, and more companionable. She was alone, to recover from flu, she said, on fresh air and home cooking. The boys had come and gone from their second stay, and were in school. Isabelle had scarlatina, with Eugenia hovering over her, so the Princess and I had to keep each other company daytimes. I'd showed her my favorite hiding places and we'd explored the whole house, even to the roof, and played games of all kinds. She never condescended, and if she was grieving, she hid her grief from me. We always had tea with Nanny. The Princess was my first friend for so long, but I knew her for such a short time.

Soon after lunch we first trooped to the drawing room. There was no place for anything to be hidden here. Amaury asked me about the not very good Raeburn of a duke's daughter who had married into the family, even though it was too large to carry. The morning room was of no interest, and the boys said they'd come back to the library later; it would take too long now to search for secret panels. Cousin Aylmer's study was unchanged, too, except that the books looked a little more worn and some of the old sets had been cleared out for rows of new titles. There were two small portraits which should have been by Holbein if the proper ancestor had had any thought for the future, but he obviously had chosen the wrong artist to do himself and his coiffed, full-blown wife. As we returned to the hall Eugenia and Alexandra began to walk together amicably and discuss antiques. The two Montlucs were impatient, consulting about every chest and cupboard, while Isabelle watched them, fascinated. Once I thought Gavin was trying to catch my eye, but I ignored him.

At the end of the corridor, opposite the study, was a door leading into the banqueting hall. Two stories high, a huge fireplace filled much of the corridor end and faced the usual musicians' gallery at the other. Another gallery ran along the courtyard wall. The draperies had been pulled back to show the rows of portraits and what linenfold paneling could be seen between them. The atmosphere tensed a bit, but as we progressed, it was evident the portraits had been there a long time, that only the family could love them, and that no second pictures had been hidden in the frames.

I lingered a minute in the long room. It had been a fine place to play on a rainy afternoon. Nanny had sometimes given us an old blanket to drape over one end of the huge table so it could be anything from a cave to a wigwam to a castle. The immense chimney had always rather awed us; we had not played around it not only because of the soot and bird nests that fell down occasionally. It was just too big and dark to be fun. I wondered if anyone went to the secret room any more.

I watched the group following Mr. Beckham back down the corridor. The whole thing, this searching through what had been my home on behalf of three men who were nothing to me, irritated me anew. I had had enough of it. I'd get my own private ramble now while the others were busy.

The corridor was open. Beyond the back courtyard ran a path through the orchards, the oak woods and the home farm. The air was soft and caressing. A lazy walk was indicated.

A hand touched my arm. "Have you had enough of it, too?" asked Gavin above me. "I thought you were looking a little annoyed."

"Yes. I was. And I hate the idea of a real search even more."

"So do I. I suppose I could stop them, but"—he shrugged—"that might make more trouble. They'd be sure, then, I was hiding something. Tell you what, Petra. Let's you and I leave them to their dirty work and go get some tea. There's a nice inn I found all by myself and I'm proud of it. It's time we said more than ten annoyed words to each other. I'm sure it won't be difficult to find pleasant ones."

For a moment I almost said No. He had behaved rudely twice, and then had ignored me. But if this was a flag of truce I should accept it. After all, he was the new heir and I was curious about him. Perhaps he'd explain the way he had acted. . . . "I'd love to go," I said, putting real warmth into my voice, and, surprisingly, without difficulty.

He backed out the rather shabby estate Morris and, when he reached the main road, turned west and north.

"Have you had time for any sightseeing?" I asked politely.

"Not yet." His hands on the steering wheel were long and hard. He could use them for anything; the car must be a toy to him after the large cars they enjoyed across the Atlantic. "I want to learn all about the estate as quickly as I can and see what needs doing. Quite a bit, I'm afraid." He glanced at me, and his gray eyes were dancing. "You don't have to ask. Yes, I can afford a certain amount without any difficulty. I saw no reason to tell the entire dinner table, but my grandfather was a good surveyor and had an eye for mineral lands, and then my father went into oil after a time at engineering. You might say I'm comfortably off, but don't tell anyone."

I laughed delightedly, and he glanced at me in surprise.

"You haven't laughed before," he said slowly. "Why now?"

"Just that I was right. I had a feeling, about your grandfather, anyway. I'm sure Eugenia has spent these three weeks trying to find out if you have a penny to your name."

"She is given to leading questions," he admitted with a small laugh of his own. "She's easy to circumvent. Alexandra's a different deal."

"Don't you find us all overwhelming?" I asked, half turning toward him in the seat.

"Yes, a little. As I said, I never had a family. My father was away a great deal. My mother died while I was in boarding school. But I find it all entertaining in several ways and somehow stabilizing to have a ready-made family. I am sure, though, few families would be as highly individual. After all, I'm very much a stranger in a strange land, and as each day passes I realize how little I know of England, her people, and, of course, of

Aylforth and what is custom and what is expediency. All of you in the family, however remote, have given me a quick induction into English ways. It's like coming into a bit of unexplored country and I find the folkways as fascinating as those of the Cree. Also, I've never been around women much. Curious creatures, aren't they?''

This was the longest and most human speech I had heard from him. It could be mulled over later. I couldn't quite believe the last part, for he had an air of complete social ease. ''No more curious than men,'' I told him with more asperity than I intended. ''And you've been around; your life hasn't been all mining camps, or wherever engineers go.''

''No,'' he admitted, still smiling. ''There was college, and Canada does have its society. But I've seen little of your sex over any period of time, and you're as interesting to watch as . . . well, as a colony of beaver.''

Again I had to laugh. ''We're industrious but not so practical? So you have been in the wilds. Where?''

He told me a little, enough to make me see plains with no limit and broken mountains reaching to the clouds. But he did not go on for long. ''Now I want to see the cities I've missed.'' He switched easily from Indians. ''Which ones do you recommend?''

''Oh, London, of course. And Paris, though I don't know it well.''

''Recently?'' I could see his eyes watching me in the mirror.

''Just three days in late May.'' Exhausting, too, full of conferences. ''Why?''

''You could tell me the newest things to see, as well as the oldest.'' He swung away from the wide road. ''And

I'd be grateful for a list of what I should see in these parts."

The Pied Horse had managed to maintain character, although it was modernized. While waiting for tea, which I insisted must include Devonshire cream for us both, in the corner of the beamed bar, Gavin led me quickly from Longleat and Stonehenge to talk about the Priory. I never had before—no one had been interested. I began cautiously, fearing to bore him, but although his figure was relaxed as he filled his pipe, his eyes turned from noncommittal to warm and interested, and his "Go on" or "Who was that?" led me into the family and my own childhood until I quite lost myself in the past and only enjoyed the tea as a secondary pleasure. I was surprised how much I could recall. But then I came to Cousin Aylmer and Nanny and the recent past and I stopped.

"You haven't said anything about London," he prodded.

"Oh, that's another story, and not so interesting." I'd talked myself out.

"Some other time, then. I'd like to hear. You've given me a feel for the Priory and the family I could never have found on my own. I'm grateful. But I haven't learned much about you." He pushed back his chair, his voice suddenly serious. "Who and what are you anyway, Petra? I don't know what to think of you. I find you . . . well . . . in one situation and then in another. At the house you're silent, or you're defending yourself against the others as if they were ganging up on you. But here, now, you're warm and gay and fun, with a touch of acid.

But you always seem alone—if you wouldn't laugh at that.''

"I wouldn't laugh," I murmured. "I have been so much. But," I went on lightly; it was not in me to go soft, "I like it that way, and I have my defenses.''

"Not always," he said with meaning. Then his face hardened. "And you certainly aren't alone the way those two Frenchmen hang around.''

The change was so sudden I jerked back in anger. "Those two? They're . . ." I bit my lip. If he could be difficult I could also. "Perhaps you are misinterpreting their good manners," I said coolly.

He was turning his pipe around on the table and didn't hear me. "You're mixed up in all this somehow. You spent a lot of time with the Princess when she was here. She might have told you something then which you didn't understand. You know so much about the house, too. I have a feeling they all believe you are hiding some special knowledge. I hope you aren't.''

"Well, I'm not. I only know about the house because Cousin Aylmer and I cared about it. As for the Montlucs . . . they're nothing.''

"Then how do you explain meeting Nico in the back lane the afternoon you arrived?''

"I didn't meet him. It was chance. I didn't even know who he was.''

"Have it your way." His tone was weary. "But if things get more than you can handle, capable at managing your affairs as you undoubtedly are, just let me know. I don't want murder and mayhem at Aylforth—for any reason, pictures or females.''

He unfolded and stalked to the bar to pay the bill. I

knew it was no good protesting, for he obviously wouldn't believe me, and that thought made me angry too. We drove back in silence. I thanked him graciously for the outing, and went upstairs. A nap was what I needed before dinner.

A scratching at the door woke me.

"Come on down, Petra," Nico was saying. "You've had your long nap. I want to walk in the woods, and I'd get lost without you. There's plenty of time."

It seemed my day for masculine attention. I might as well complete the roster and see what this one would say. "Meet you downstairs in five minutes," I called. I might as well give Gavin something real to think about, if he saw us.

We went out through the walled garden and along the path beyond the orchards. The woods were all green and gold and peaceful, except for Nico. First he told me, half angrily, no hiding place with pictures had been found. Then he started on their visits as boys. I knew where he was heading.

"Look." I stopped and faced him. "I don't remember a thing I haven't told already about the time you arrived. Amaury has asked me also, so there's no use asking me again. I'm sick of the subject. Tell me about Paris."

He did, with gaiety and enthusiasm. It was a Paris of parties that lasted to dawn, and of racing at Longchamp and Auteuil, and of house parties and hunts. It sounded like a French version of *Sketch,* and fun, for a little while.

As we neared the spring in the glade where sometimes we saw deer, I put a hand on his arm and shushed him. He nodded and we stole forward, but there was nothing but a cock pheasant stepping across the upper end. He scuttled when I yelled and flapped my arms, which pleased me.

"Go on," I told Nico. "I like hearing about things that are strange and new."

He was staring at the spring, his face a mask, then whirled and seized my shoulders. "Petra, you *must* know something. The pictures must be here. I—we—must find them." There was a queer intent look in his eyes. I knew he was going to cover his seriousness by kissing me and stepped back before he could. "I know nothing," I answered brusquely, "and I'm no help to you."

I started to the lane, and he followed sullenly. I began to wonder. Was this why I could never shake both the Frenchmen? But that was ridiculous; it was just that they were being polite guests.

Behind me he said, "Very well. But if you do think of anything useful, it is *me* you tell, remember that." It sounded too much like a threat for the smooth Montluc, and he knew it and tried to chuckle, not very successfully. "I'm counting on you, my girl."

I wanted to point out I was no one's girl, but instead ignored him, and he could find nothing to say, not even when we passed the gap in the wall where we had met. Around the curve, in a field that had once belonged to a farmer named Catchpenny, was a small trailer. A man sitting on the step was mending a pot.

"It isn't often one sees tinkers now," I observed and looked back. From under his black hat the man was watching us. I had distinctly heard Nico say, "One inside and one out." Was this the one outside, and why? And who was inside?

I tried to be pleased with myself when Gavin came down early for dinner as we strolled into the front hall. But I wasn't, really.

We played bridge that night, two tables, thanks to Roger, and suddenly everyone was gay and relaxed. We kept changing, cutting for partners at the end of each rubber. All played well; Nico, I thought, was quite professional, but even Roger, in his slow, careful way was formidable. It was the third rubber that I found myself paired with Gavin against Isabelle and Nico. For the first time I was nervous, and right away made an error from which he rescued me unobtrusively and gracefully. But he looked patient about it and that annoyed me. I made myself relax and suddenly knew I was playing well above my usual form. We settled down to it. Nico and Isabelle moved into top form, too, and it became more serious.

Once, when I was dummy, I found myself scanning my partner. He looked, well, elegant in the dinner jacket, his shoulders just broad enough for his slender height. I'd never let myself study him before. With his eyes downcast on his cards, I could see how thick the black lashes were. He had good, wide-set cheekbones, and his jawline and chin were certainly firm. He'll be just as handsome when he's eighty, I told myself with surprise. He looked up to that moment, caught my glance and gave me a wink, then ended the game by a brilliant play with the five of spades and won the rubber for us. We all murmured politely how much we had enjoyed the game. He nodded at me carelessly. ''We're good partners.

We must play together again," but turned away as we rose.

Isabelle drifted beside me. "Do you think the Princess could have given anything to Cousin Aylmer to keep for her?" she asked. Her voice was languid, but there was an intent look in her eyes. "Gavin maintains there's nothing in the study, and we could find nothing in the safe there."

"If she did he would have put it in the bank," I answered. "He wouldn't keep anything so valuable in the house. And he'd see the Princess got back whatever it was as soon as possible."

"You're probably right." She faked a yawn. "I just wondered . . ." And she floated away in the general direction of Nico.

So she and Gavin had been searching together, I thought sourly. Well, Isabelle never found anything she mislaid herself; she wouldn't find anything anyone else had hidden.

6

But Isabelle's question kept nagging at me, even when I was in bed. Anything valuable entrusted to Cousin Aylmer he would surely have taken to the bank, and there would be a record. But another person? The secret room was something else again. I had myself shown it to the Princess, she had said it reminded her of the one in the castle in Hungary. Isabelle and I had been taken there once by Cousin Aylmer, but as far as I knew, she never went again because of the dust and spiders. But I'd gone back, though not often; it was too scary, and Nanny at last, finding bread and water for supper did not keep me away, had asked me not to hide there because it frightened her. But I knew the way in and out. Anything could be hidden there.

Why not go there now and see? Too many people were around in the daytime, and it was no one's business what I did. And I admitted it would be gratifying if the blasted pictures were there and I could confound the family.

In the black of night the Priory went back through the

centuries. It was the Tudor stones holding the house, I always felt; they had endured so long. Even though I knew better, I always felt them crowding around the rooms. Nothing Cousin Aylmer said could convince me the place was not haunted; I knew I had felt a waft of air on my cheek more than once, heard a rustle that was not mice but a silken gown, sensed a presence that was not there. It all scared me, a little, but I was immune to real fear because the debonair Simon Templar beside me laughed at such notions. At first he had led me, seeking the spy or the thief of the moment, and as he was silent I was silent, and soon I could slip around the house without a sound. After a while, when I could find my way without using my torch, it was I who led him. Sometimes he was transformed into a dashing Pimpernel on a secret mission from France, or he became a wounded cavalier, hiding after Marston Moor. I only allowed myself an hour on these excursions so I would not look too wan in the morning and suffer a dose of physic from Nanny. Once in a while I wondered if Cousin Aylmer knew of my wanderings and imaginings, but if he did he never gave me away.

As I eased open the door of the nursery and closed it behind me, I was once more the twelve-year-old, and the Saint was waiting in the corridor. I was rather glad he was, for twenty-five feels differently about creeping through a house when all have gone to bed. I told myself firmly he was beside me, was grateful for the thick carpeting, scorned to use my torch and avoided the carved dower chest against the wall. There was moonlight in the center courtyard, and the tall windows on the stairs brought it inside so the white marble gleamed and the crystals of the chandelier became a cluster of stars. I had forgotten how lovely the hall could be. Only the thought of my errand took me into the blackness of the side hall and to the banqueting room. I had always gone to the secret room this way to avoid passing Cousin Aylmer's bedroom on the second floor.

In the banqueting hall there were sounds, but I could account for them all; a mouse in the wall, a bat in the chimney, a creak from an aged chair. The light from the row of windows made navigation easy. The door to the stairs beside the fireplace opened by a handle in the carving, and though the stairs were a thick black when I closed the door, I still would not use the torch until I reached the landing, where the steps turned.

The room was probably not really secret in the early days of the house, just a convention in all Tudor mansions, for anyone who measured could find telltale space between the back of the great fireplace and the wall of the second-floor corridor. But the room had been used. Muskets and swords had been stored here at the time of Charles I (they had been found and sold as antiques long ago), and there had been chests for the unseemly finery of Sir Kenelm Langlade's wife when Cromwell's men were looking for vanities. Fugitives had been hidden, the last time during the 1715 uprising, Cousin Aylmer had told me. I had always been sure smugglers had known of it, and perhaps even a highwayman or so. He had agreed it was possible, and let me keep a silver shoe buckle I found behind a chest. I still had it.

When I had come there as a child, carrying a flickering candle, the shadows had frightened me, now my torch was more effective, and the shadows were smaller.

On one side of the ten-foot square space loomed the heavy stones of the chimney, and I could see the black cover of the flue that brought in fresh air. Oddly enough, in spite of the thick walls and the silence, it was no longer an unfriendly place. One advantage of added years, I told myself.

Just as I remembered, the two chests stood side by side, deep and wide and long enough for a man to lie on, and empty. In that bare, stone-enclosed room there was no other place to hide anything. I was more sure than ever the pictures had never come to Aylforth.

"Trespassing again, Petra? Or is this just snooping and prying?" The voice was as friendly as an ice cube. Gavin had had to stoop as he came through the door, and when he straightened he seemed to reach to the ceiling. He was in shirt sleeves, and I thought inconsequentially how effective the tanned skin was against the white. He pushed the door closed.

I turned the torch down to the floor. "I'm not trespassing or snooping," I told him in a voice I hoped was equally cold, "and you know it. Must you always be so insufferable? How did you find me?"

"I use these little stairs when I work late in the study. I was coming up when I saw the light through a crack in the panel; the door was not closed tightly. Why are you here . . . now?"

"Isabelle asked me where Cousin Aylmer might have put something entrusted to him. She said you and she had found nothing in the safe. And that made me think of this place."

"Yes. Isabelle wished to look in the safe herself, and

was satisfied. I did not tell her Beckham and I had gone through it my first day. There is nothing here?''

He took the torch from me and moved around, looking behind the chests and in them and sat down. ''Tell me about this,'' he invited, almost cordially. ''Who else knows?''

''Isabelle—if she remembers,'' I allowed unwillingly. ''Perhaps Mr. Beckham, but Cousin Aylmer might have thought it too unimportant to mention. Alexandra and Eugenia probably saw it years ago.''

''But your cousin showed it to you?''

''One rainy afternoon when we were young and bored.'' I recounted the bits I could recall. He was watching me above the circle of light on the floor.

''So I might never have known of it except for you,'' he observed when I finished. ''This time I will take back my words. But you'll get in trouble yet, child, if you dash about on your own like this and with so many of my other new cousins here looking for something.'' His voice was mocking.

I ignored that. ''Why is Isabelle so concerned?''

''It will have something to do with her, you may be sure. She is self-centered, as you are, but prefers a minimum of effort to get what she wants. You go after things hard, like a man.''

I did not care to think we were alike at all. ''We have had different lives,'' I said coolly, ''but if I thought there was any use I'd certainly go on looking.''

''You will not. For many reasons. I forbid it.''

That was an order, and I was never one to take orders. ''I will do as I please, and you can't stop me.''

I reached for the torch and his fingers closed over my

wrist. "No?" he asked softly. I could not move my hand. "I could, you know, if I wished." The band of his fingers tightened and fell away.

I snatched up the torch, and he unfolded his long legs and rose. "Show me how to open the door, each side," he ordered.

There had been such tension in that momentary clasp of his hand that I was shaken. Without a word I pointed to the carvings on both sides. He took the torch and kept fingering and trying the springs until he was satisfied, while I grew annoyed at being kept waiting.

On the landing he thrust the torch in my hand. "Go back to your room and don't go wandering again at night."

I pulled the door closed by the carved pomegranate in the center and put out the torch. I didn't need it, and I half hoped he'd fall down the steps. But I heard nothing as I opened the door into the upstairs hall and started to the front of the house.

I had taken perhaps ten steps down the hall (the Saint was no longer with me, I realized afterward, and in my preoccupation with that last scene I had forgotten his precepts) when a cloth came down over my head and I was jerked to a halt. Hands opened mine quickly; the torch fell and was kicked away; hands went into the pockets of my peignoir and came out. I was shoved back against the wall, then a movement of air showed that whoever it was had left.

My hands were shaking as I lifted the pillowcase from my head. My torch. If I could find it I could see who had done this. The hall was long: no door had opened. I got down on my knees to feel in the blackness and knew, with anger, that I could not find it in time. Who had dared to touch me, to search my pockets?

A light sprang at me. "There's nothing under the rug for you to find," Gavin said wearily above me. "I've had them up and cleaned. Or is it another panel? Don't try to explain." Then, with quick anger, "I told you to go to your room."

I sat up. "I was going when someone put *that* over my head." I pointed to the pillowcase, white at the edge of the light. "He . . . he knocked my torch away and searched my pockets. At least he didn't hit me—this time." I was nearly stammering with outrage.

Gavin swept his own light about and found my torch at the other side of the hall. He picked it up, then the pillowcase, then me, with one hand under my elbow. "Some day you'll learn there's no honor among thieves. I'll take care of the pillowcase. We'll forget about it. Go along."

I went, his light following me as far as the corner.

I thought my anger, divided between Gavin and the unknown, would keep me tossing, but it didn't. I slept long and well.

In the morning I went to Salisbury. Driving is always soothing, and I began to tell myself I was unduly alarmed by the incident in the hall last night, and by other incidents I could have brought to mind and didn't, and there was no need to disturb Mr. Thetwin. As for Gavin, I could wish he weren't so attractive, and so strange—friendly one moment and hostile the next. Then I caught the first glimpse of that slender spire that is one of the loveliest things in England, and somehow

Return to Aylforth 88

questions were banished. I had forgotten how green meadows could be and how stately the trees, and that the Avon, when I came to it, flowed as gently as the sweet Afton.

There was a new parking place by the cathedral. I could spare five minutes, I told myself, and went inside the close just to gaze at the soaring walls and spire. Next I made a point of passing the King's Arms because I had always cherished the inn where desperate and gallant royalists had gathered to plan for the escape of Charles after Worcester. So I was quite myself when I found the offices of Mr. Thetwin in one of a row of brick houses on New Street, small cheerful rooms like Mr. Thetwin himself.

Of course I should have remembered him, for he had come occasionally to the Priory. He was kind and friendly and spoke just once, briefly, of Cousin Aylmer. It was fortunate the place had fallen into such able hands, he went on, for Mr. Gavin had a good business head and was a very competent man in every way; he could even repair a tenant's tractor, it was said.

"Also it is fortunate that Mr. Gavin need not stint on the repairs; he has assured me he can take care of many of them immediately. The estate tax is large by itself, and the farms eat up money now, so much was let go during the war and after. Your dear cousin would never sell any land, and the tenants knew he took care of them as best as he could, but now things will be even better for them."

Again remembering Isabelle, I asked if Cousin Aylmer had ever entrusted a package or left anything to be held. No, only Mrs. McLennan had given him anything to

. . . . *89*

keep—as I knew—a will, a bankbook and a key. The will was brought in and I saw that indeed Nanny had bequeathed a tin truck stored in the attic and the money in the savings account—247 pounds, 14 shillings, 3 pence. I signed for the key and left the bankbook and will and promised to call on Mr. Thetwin at any time he could be of service. We shook hands in real friendship.

In the back lane a black car passed me and drew up by the caravan. The tinker did rather well by himself, I thought.

At lunch Cousin Alexandra, smiling happily, announced she was taking the four young people to call on her dear friend Jane, now the widowed Lady Clareham. It was many years, she told us, since she had had such a handsome group to display, and she intended to make all her friends envious. Gavin and Eugenia were not included.

There was never any arguing with Cousin Alexandra, and we dressed obediently and were driven in her limousine to Clareham Castle, quite an hour into the next county. When Alexandra wished to be charming she was, and she made the whole expedition entertaining. We all talked, about the Priory and what we remembered of our childhood, Isabelle preening herself a trifle because she was younger and had not shared our exploits, and of England and how it had changed and the difficulties of living comfortably in the present.

Clareham Castle turned out to be a modest Georgian house with a ruined keep on the grounds. Dear Jane was wispy, with two unmarried wispy daughters to whom the boys were charming over tea. There were some vague young men and girls around to whom Alexandra paid no attention. After tea we admired the rose garden and the keep from a distance, and a small and not difficult maze, and I noticed Alexandra strolling first with one Montluc and then the other. King Edward would have said she was a fine figure of a woman, and though she was dressed in a rather severe yellow crepe I could see her billowing and frothy with a parasol to twirl. Her auburn hair had been famous, and that, her cheerful disposition and her determination, had found her two wealthy husbands who had adored her. Isabelle attached a slightly robust young man and I one who gangled. Lady Jane watched everything carefully, and I had a feeling she would get those girls married yet.

As we were going down the steps to the car, a white-haired, white-moustached man, a complete colonel although without a uniform, was arriving. Alexandra inclined her head graciously and smiled at him, which froze him to a military stance before he bowed in return. In the car mirror I could see him watching us.

Alexandra made a little moue. "I am sure that was Dudley Campion. He's a baronet now and something in the county. He should have recognized me even though it's years since we met."

I was sure she wanted to turn around and look back, but she settled comfortably again into the role of hostess.

We disposed of Clareham quickly on the way back and settled down to amuse ourselves again. This time we talked of France, which Alexandra seemed to know, and the joys of Paris. Amaury sulked until he was asked about Normandy and then would have bored us endlessly with his farming problems, but we reached home before he was well launched. We thanked Alexandra, and she warned us she would take off again if there was time.

Gavin appeared at dinner, correct and formal as always. We did not speak. Tomorrow I would open Nanny's trunk and do her errands and then leave, I decided. I had had enough of Aylforth.

First there was the evening to get through. Gavin bowed himself away, so there was no chance of bridge, though Eugenia made futile clucking sounds about it. Before we could sort ourselves out, Alexandra took my arm and led the way to a couch by the far windows, settling herself in one corner. "I haven't had a chance to talk to you yet. Tell me all about yourself."

Usually that means the person wishes you to listen submissively to his or her own fascinating life, but the look she gave me was kindly. I was tempted. No one had yet asked me what I had done with my years. Long ago I made it a habit not to talk about Petra Norreys to anyone, but once in a while we all of us hope we will find one person truly interested who will really wish to hear our remarkable deeds and thoughts. But even as I hesitated she began.

"Why did you never come to me for help after you ran away? I would have helped. You were silly not to."

If she could be frank, so could I. I looked squarely into her quite lovely brown eyes. "It never occurred to me you would help. After all, I had only seen you at a distance, and you had never made the slightest gesture toward me except for a few kind words once in a while."

The heavy white lids blinked once. "You are quite right, of course," she answered calmly. "I wasn't interested in you as a child, though I was fond of the thought of you because of your parents. I never cared for children other than my own, so I made no effort about you. I assumed you were happy and well and forgot you. But when you disappeared and no one knew where you were I was concerned."

"You did nothing," I pointed out.

She nodded. "I did not see what I could do. I just hoped you would come to me sometime. Aylmer was worried."

"Yes. That bothered me. But as soon as I had a job and could truthfully say I was all right, I let him know. And after that I did write, quite often. And I did come down."

The auburn head that was graying so skillfully (or the gray head that was touched with auburn) bent a little. "Yes. You came when he was alone, which he appreciated, and understood. He told me. What happened, Petra, that sent you off in a rage? He never knew."

"Naturally. It would have bothered him. It was made quite clear to me, one morning"—in spite of myself my glance flicked to Eugenia—"that I had outstayed my welcome and that I was too expensive a luxury for him to support longer. The case in point was the school bill for the next term which had just arrived. After all, I was a very distant Langlade indeed, with no claim to charity. I always knew I had no money of my own, but I had not realized a penniless child was such a burden, practically taking the bread from Cousin Aylmer's mouth—and Eugenia's, I was told." I knew I sounded bitter but could not help it. "And all done as if he had said it, so I could not go to him and ask—anything."

"Both you and Eugenia were stupid," Alexandra said

calmly. "You should have known her better than to believe her. Isabelle's debut was ahead, and she was saving every penny. Aylmer never blamed you because your parents died before your father could make any money. Your parents were intelligent, delightful people, and Aylmer and I loved them both. Aylmer had hopes for you, after school . . . Cambridge perhaps. He always said you were the most intelligent of the family. He was disappointed when you left."

"I know." This time it was I who blinked. But at least—I hugged the thought to myself—he knew his affection and care had not been wasted, for I told him of my small triumphs. He couldn't have been too disappointed last year.

"Eugenia, now," Alexandra continued, "was once mildly pretty and had some money of her own. My brother was a handsome man, as you can tell by looking at Isabelle, with no head for figures, or much of anything except soldiering. He ran through his own money and much of Eugenia's. After his death she accepted Aylmer's support, for all these years, as her right. Her small funds are managed well, but she has always saved every penny to put on Isabelle so she might lead the kind of life Eugenia thinks is proper and that will ultimately find her a wealthy husband."

"She shouldn't have begrudged me my only home," I burst out. "I'll never forget the nights in the city when I cried from homesickness and loneliness and just plain fear."

"But that is Eugenia, greedy and without imagination," the warm voice sympathized. "You were too young to realize. Probably that resentment you cherish drove you hard. And she does have her crosses—herself and the unmarried Isabelle."

"Why *unmarried?*" Curiosity lightened bitterness.

The ample white shoulders shrugged. "They both hope for bigger game than they have found. The trouble with Isabelle is that she appears selfish and cold; any intelligent man will shy away, and the unintelligent seek larger fortunes. And I imagine no man has ever reached her heart. But, about you . . . you look very well, Petra, aside from looking tired, and not too *gamine,* which could have been a danger because of your curls and figure. What *did* you do with yourself?"

"I became a secretary," I began cautiously.

If Alexandra had had a fan she would have tapped my wrist approvingly. "There. You *are* intelligent. Did you stay one?"

"For quite a while because I wanted to learn—many things. Then I started on my own, and that worked, so then I went on to something else, and that worked too."

"Closemouthed little thing, aren't you?" My cousin was amused. "Well, tell me when you wish; I'd like to hear. So few of our family have made any money. Now I'm going to talk to Nico." She called him over, and having no mind for a threesome, I went up to my room.

I had been given a glimpse of myself I did not like, and I should examine it. Had it really been resentment and, yes, at times when the going was worse, even hatred of Eugenia and Isabelle that had driven me to my mild success? All my childhood Eugenia had been the black witch, ignoring or punishing me and pushing forward the child with golden hair. Nanny had done her best to shield me from what I had thought was hatred and was probably malice and irritation. But if those were my feelings, perhaps they had affected me, put me more on the defensive than was necessary. Was I really without charity? No, I answered quickly, I wasn't; kindness to others had always seemed important to me, but perhaps it had been too careless a kindness. I could excuse my childhood feelings and blame them on youth and lack of experience. But now? Perhaps the detachment that I had cultivated and cherished, that had enabled me to watch people and use them, had been an outgrowth of my dislike of any involvement. Keeping all at a distance had been useful, but perhaps I had carried it too far. Well, it wasn't likely I'd change.

On bare feet I padded to the closet to hang my dinner dress. As I lifted down the hanger I heard a door close and a muffled sentence, and a word that sounded like my name. The two Montlucs were in that room. What were they saying about me?

If I had exaggerated when I had said that first night that I knew all the stones of the Priory, I at least knew where they were not, and where thin walls had been put in place of sturdy ones when rooms had been remodeled. Space for two closets had been taken from the large bedroom next to the nursery on the right, making ample space for shelves and racks. Each closet was half the width of the rooms. Once, when I was old enough to have the nursery to myself, two very distant, elderly cousins had come to visit for a few days and had been given the adjoining bedchamber. While hanging up my dress that evening I had heard their voices almost clearly. The door of their closet, I had decided, was open and the sound was coming through it and through the thin partition between the two. Here was something Raffles, or perhaps, by now, the Baron, would use! With my penknife I had made a hole in the thin wood of the partition, and then I could hear every word that was said. But they had only been discussing the vicar and his wife, who had been at dinner, and that soon bored me. Laboriously I had filled in the hole with the plug I had cut out, and it had never been noticed. I had not used it again, for my conscience told me eavesdropping was only justified in time of danger, and that had never come.

Curiosity had often taken me into trouble, and now the temptation was too much, though I could almost hear Nanny saying eavesdroppers seldom heard good of themselves. My fingers found the old unevenness, and my nails worked at the plug until it was loose. Yes, the door of the other closet must be open, for I could hear distinctly.

"It's that Perdita we must watch," a voice was saying. It was Manson, not at all suave. "She said there at table she knew every bit of the house. She's too clever by half. Was out of her room last night, too."

"How do you know?" Amaury's voice was sharp.

"Was out myself, just looking around. Saw her come up the little stairs. She hadn't found anything, though."

"Isabelle probably knows as much about the place."

"Not that one. She doesn't bestir herself about such things as the house. I've watched her for two weeks now."

"And in those two weeks you haven't found any place yourself where the pictures could be hidden."

Manson growled something about not having enough

time to himself, always someone at him, and he couldn't see much in the dark.

"We'll have to find out what Petra knows, then," Nico cut in. "We can make her tell us."

"Here, now, nothing's going to happen to Petra. I won't allow that." Amaury was just as decisive. "I don't see why you're so sure the bloody pictures are here anyway."

"Our-er-people found out that one of the Montluc pictures was sold in London in 1941—all very hush, hush, no name of buyer or seller, but it is certain. We don't make mistakes about things like that. And I told you about that book."

"Yes." Amaury hadn't liked the tone. "But that was all very indefinite. Just said Mother had helped the Free French, which everyone knew anyway. It may have been with the jewels, you know."

"We're quite sure they went too. But we could figure no other way a picture from Montmézay could have reached the London market at that time. I agree with Manson. We must watch Petra. Louis can follow anyone who leaves the Priory, for any of these people might be helping her, and Manson and you and I can watch her here."

"I don't much like all this business," Amaury said slowly. "I want to find the pictures and so does Uncle, or I wouldn't have come along with you on this chase. And we wouldn't have believed you except for the letter coming from the lawyer just after Cousin Aylmer died. Mother obviously did leave something here, but it must have been the jewels, and she must have come later and taken them away. There was no date on the note, you saw that, and it just said she or Maxim would come and ask Aylmer's advice about a problem. You and I could have been that problem.''

''If she meant the jewels, why didn't she leave them in a bank in London?''

''Some banks had moved their deposit boxes out in the country—too hard for her to get to them. Those still in the city might get bombed. She was probably afraid someone else would get their hands on whatever it was if anything happened to her. This must have been the safest place she knew.'' Amaury was quite positive. ''But Petra's a nice girl—prickly, but nice. She'll tell me if she finds anything, and I promise I'll tell you.''

Nico snickered. ''She better. Or, as I said, we'll make her . . . of course in a nice way.'' But his tone was almost vicious.

''All right. You stay with her, or one of us will be on guard.'' Manson's voice moved away. ''Can't trust a female anyway.''

Steps were coming toward the closet. Frantically I pushed the plug back in place and tried not to breathe. There was a rustle and click and the door closed. I crept back into my room. I'd heard enough, and yet, really not enough. The Montlucs were certainly going after things in a professional way. Where could they have found a person like Manson to work with them? He was experienced, and if the pictures did turn up, it would be the professionals, the people behind him, who would make off with the canvases. I could be sure of that. But if they were not found soon there was that threat of Nico's that he would make me tell—in a *nice* way. And I couldn't make anyone believe I knew nothing! Also, no one would believe what I had just heard. But if, by some extraordinary chance, the pictures were found here, I would *have* to tell about the three men and their conversation to save the pictures from thieves. I was the only one who knew—I couldn't leave Aylforth. Anyway—and an icy finger ran down my spine—the Montlucs and Manson wouldn't let me.

7

Cousin Eugenia's discipline about breakfast had quite broken down by now, and people came as they wished. Amaury was leaving as I entered, and Nico arrived as I finished. I walked out and on into a luminous belt of mist beneath the beeches. I might go for a long walk, or I might take the car and drive all day. No, I couldn't, not after what I had heard last night. They'd stop me, somehow. But I could go to Nanny's trunk and do her errands, and then that, at least, would be behind me. I went back to the house and said good morning politely to Eugenia, who was in the front hall spoiling a huge bunch of delphiniums, all blues and beautiful, and upstairs to Susan as she came out of my room. The key of the trunk was in my change purse, and the house was quiet as I took the upper hall of the right wing.

The stairs to the attic were behind an unobtrusive door whose black latch and bolt hardly showed against the dark wood. Before going up the boxed-in stairs, without thought, I slid the inside bolt in place as we always had so there would be some warning of Nanny's approach. For some forgotten reason, hidden by centuries, the attic of the left wing had never been properly floored, and this attic on the right wing had always been the one used.

As I came up on the wide-planked floor I sniffed the familiar scent of old wood and musty cloth, a faint potpourri from long-abandoned jars, ancient wood smoke and bats. Isabelle had not objected to the attic, and we had sometimes played here happily, dragging out ancient and forgotten garments from chests and trunks, canes from a collection in the corner, even looking through piles of magazines someone had once cherished. There was plenty of light from the square casement windows set in the gables.

Someone had done some cleaning out, for the magazines were gone, and the trunks and chests were empty except for one which held a mass of blackout curtains and another which held our collection of dolls and animals. That must have been Nanny's doing. Even after I had outgrown dolls I had sneaked up here once in a while to play with my favorites, and find some sort of comfort from their familiar battered faces. And there, facing the stairs, was Nanny's solidly square trunk. I dragged it forward.

It was full almost to the top, and I remembered Nanny's saying she had saved things she intended to mend or do over and then never had. On top of a woolen bathrobe lay an envelope, "For Petra," which held Nanny's will and the list of bequests:

"Mrs. Mellowfield has already received her garnet brooch.

"To Mrs. Springer at the Post, the cairngorm pin she has always admired.

"To Mrs. Cowdry at Twin Oaks farm, my watch.

"To Mrs. Whalley at the Sweets Shop, the gold pin with the pearl.

"To Mrs. Carrick at the Oak and Thorn, the circle of amethysts the Princess gave me and the picture of the cottage."

Each gift, except the picture, was in a little white box with the name on top. Four gifts to bestow; that would not take long, though I would have to find Mrs. Carrick. They would all be pleased; they were nice women and had been good friends to Nanny. I could start this afternoon.

Beside the boxes was an envelope of Cousin Aylmer's stationery and inside a note. "The things that belong to me in this trunk are left in the care of my friend Mrs. McLennan and my cousin Aylmer Langlade, who will know what can best be done about them if I or my representative do not return to claim them." It was signed by the Princess with her full name.

I wondered, mildly, what sort of clothes she had left. I would have to get them out and ask Cousin Alexandra what to do about them. And I must take the fine new bathrobe back to London to keep me warm winter nights.

The faintest of sounds, or perhaps it was only a feeling, made me raise my eyes and look down the stairs to the door. It trembled ever so slightly, and I saw the black latch lift and fall back noiselessly. I held my breath. The bolt would hold, but the door could be broken down by weight, or an ax. There was another echo of a sound and then nothing. Whoever it was, and it could have been anyone, was gone. Anger followed fear, and I hurried across and down the steps. Perhaps this time I could glimpse the unknown. I slid back into the bolt and lifted the latch, but the door did not move. I was quite firmly locked in. He—she—it—must have known I was there as soon as the door was found locked. Anger and fear joined and then faded. I must use my wits and not my emotions.

Of course I could escape. It wouldn't be the first time I had gone out the back window and up over the gable and roof and down the holds left by the builders to the roof of the stables and then down the ladder against the far wall. The slates of the roofs were only slippery if wet, and I was still thin enough to get through the window. I took out the boxes and letters and put them on top of the trunk, locked it and put the key in the button-down pocket of my blouse and put my shoes beside the boxes. I looked at the envelopes again. There was a copy of the will but not of the document from the Princess. It had been written, I was sure, to protect Nanny in case Cousin Eugenia said she had no right to give away what the Princess had left behind, and to bring in Cousin Aylmer's authority in case of need. But whoever had locked me in would be coming some time to see what I had been after in the attic. If I took the papers with me and fell, they would be found and questions begun. I looked around. The dust motes glinted in wide paths from the windows to the bare floor.

The chests were too obvious a hiding place, but . . . In ignominious exile below the dolls was Winnie, my beloved teddy bear. A side seam had been ripped in some game, and I had closed it with a safety pin. Nanny had said I must sew it, and I refused; I hated sewing; and when she said I could not play with him until he was properly put together I had brought him to the attic. His black button eyes were as bright as ever and his black nose as engagingly tilted. The rusty pin came out at last, and there was the long slit. I had to take out some of the stuffing before I could slide the envelope with the two sheets into the stuffing and press them flat, and the inexpert restuffing gave him an odd shape, but the pin closed the gap again. My fingers were shaking when I finished. At first I thought to leave him in the chest, but now that seemed to shout it was a hiding place. So I took him and Elizabeth, my favorite doll because she had brown hair like mine, over to the farthest corner, where the stand still held a collection of old canes, and dropped them behind it. One of the blackout cloths covered them both nicely, and the heap vanished into the shadows.

The second window above the courtyard was the one I had used before. What I had done ten years ago I could do again, I told myself, and tugged back the window. My shoulders were somewhat broader, I found, and I had to go through at a slant and then twist to catch hold of the top of the frame, but I could draw out one leg and plant it on the ledge and then the other, and then I was on top of the gable with the slanting slates rising to the peak of the roof. I found I did not have quite my former insouciance as I straddled the roof and edged to the end to look for the holds down the corner—what age does to one! I thought sadly—but the uneven stones were there amid ivy grown thicker, and they were amply wide for my feet and hands. I came down quickly, not looking at anything but dusty leaves and the inevitable spiders, and landed on the gentle slope of the long stable. This time I did not try to balance my way along the ridge, but my feet clung safely to the slates and so to the ladder, long fastened to the outer wall. On the ground, I dusted my hands. Well, someone had been fooled, but for how long? I must get back to the attic for my shoes, but with no unseemly haste. There could be eyes anywhere. The scullery door might be best. . . .

As I turned the corner into the stableyard, a shadow loomed above me. "This time I at least do you the courtesy of asking what you have lost," said Gavin. Hair ruffled, eyes searching, he was bending forward above a black horse. "And why should it be on the roof?"

"And why should you be following me?" I demanded angrily.

His lips twitched. "Following you? My dear Petra, you flatter me and my horse. I can take Black Peter most places, but not on those slates."

"Then why are you here, and now?" I was echoing his own words and did not care if he recognized them or not.

"In a faint hope to be here in case you fell. I was coming by the side lane and could hardly miss a figure on top of one of the gables. I knew it could only be you. Did you find anything?"

"Someone locked me in the attic." Now I was annoyed at myself for that stupid question I'd asked.

"Really?" The glint left his eyes and the tone was coolly disbelieving. "Perhaps you had better show me."

He tied Peter and took my elbow and led me along the walk to the small door. Without heels on I felt ridiculously small, which annoyed me further, and also that he knew the halls and stairs as well as I did. At the attic door I stepped back and pointed. He lifted the latch and the door swung open.

There was anger in his eyes as he swung on me. "Once more I ask you what game you are playing. I don't believe you were ever here."

"My shoes will prove that." I pushed by him and up the stairs. The shoes still stood on the trunk, with the list and the little boxes, but someone had been there. The shoes were further to the left and the tops of two boxes were not fitted tightly, as though they had been closed in haste.

"I'll concede the evidence of the shoes," he admitted, "but not the locking in. It's another of your tricks. What are those?"

I snatched up the list and thrust it at him. He read it carefully; his gray eyes when he lifted them, were curious. "This list is from your Nanny? I had one who had the same sort of handwriting." His voice gentled. "It was to do this for her you really came back, Petra?"

"Yes, of course." I would not give in an inch. "The last time I saw her she said she had some errands for me, some day, whenever I came down again."

"And this?" His toe touched the trunk.

"Her trunk. Full of her old clothes. She saved everything."

"Ummmm." He rubbed one jawbone. "In one thing, anyway, I have done you an injustice. I did not know it was affection brought you back."

"You really know nothing at all," I told him hotly. "Of course it was affection, for Cousin Aylmer and Nanny. I had no idea I would find such a conglomeration of people here—or the new master.''

He moved and opened each box. "I am sure of that," he tossed back. "If you will put on your shoes we might look at this picture, and then you are quite free to do those errands.''

One shoe was on and I stamped it, hard, on the floor and had to catch the trunk to save my balance. "Of course I'm free to, and you and no one can stop me. I'll show you that picture, since you don't trust me.''

My heels clattered on the stairs. In Nanny's room I lifted down the water color of the cottage. He carried it to the window and his face softened. "I noticed this before. It's quite nice, you know, with real feeling. No wonder she left it to a Scotch friend. Very well.''

He handed it to me and I hung it back. "I hope you're satisfied now, about *everything*," I said haughtily as I swished out of the door. Back in my room I found it had been searched, not quite expertly enough. Was that why I had been locked in?

At luncheon I told them all, casually, that I would be doing my errands in the village in the afternoon. I could feel their eyes intent on me as I went on about Nanny and her bequests.

"Where did she keep them?" Eugenia interrupted before I was through. "I didn't find any jewelry. . . ." Her voice died away self-consciously. I felt such anger at the thought of her going through Nanny's things that I could barely answer civilly.

"In the tin trunk Cousin Aylmer gave her to hold her clothes and her quilt and the knitted afghan her mother had made." I sent her one furious glance and then looked back at my plate. I could feel a relaxing around the table. A tin trunk holding a nurse's old clothes was of little interest.

"I remember that afghan," Isabelle said surprisingly. "She used to wrap you in it when you came in all wet from one of your ploys. It was all different shades of green."

Surprise and pleasure that she had remembered damped back my fury and made me smile at her. For the first time she actually smiled back, and quite nicely. I knew Gavin was looking at us both, and ignored him.

"Are there any errands I can do?" I asked, to round off the topic.

There weren't. Amaury offered to come with me, but withdrew when I said I would have to stay and talk to all the recipients and it would probably take hours.

It did take hours, particularly Mrs. Whalley. She and Nanny had been quite close, so I had to hear more than I wished of her last months after her heart attack, when Mrs. Whalley had often gone up to the house to see her. But, I was assured, she had been quiet and content and often spoke of me with the affection she had usually kept hidden until that last visit. We both shed a few tears and recovered our spirits over strong tea, and I left with more of a feeling of peace than I had had.

The other visits were brief, but I'd have to go to Downleigh some fifteen miles away to find Mrs. Carrick, now living with her son. It was too late then, so I went back by the lanes and passed the caravan. They really did themselves well, I thought, for I noticed they were hooked up to the electric line as well as to the telephone.

It seemed vaguely illegal, but I supposed there were ways of getting around inconvenient rules.

Roger turned up for tea and asked us all to a swim and picnic on the shore the next day. He promised a lunch and the private beach of a friend away from trippers and tea. It was warm enough, and the idea appealed. But that meant a trip to Salisbury the next morning for a bathing suit, for it had not occurred to me to bring one. It also meant putting off the visit to Mrs. Carrick, but that could wait.

We were standing around uncertainly after the coffee that evening when Nico turned on the wireless in the corner and found dance music. Quite properly, he returned and bowed to Eugenia, who practically simpered as she shook her head. Alexandra also declined, and then, smooth dark head bent above the golden one, he was guiding Isabelle to the hall, where there was plenty of room; Amaury had seized my hand impatiently. He was a competent if slightly too-French-in-manner dancer, and I had plenty of time to watch the other two. Isabelle was flushed and alive, her eyes sparkled, and she actually giggled at something and then was silent. They were a handsome pair, but so were we, and in a handsome setting. The huge chandelier glittered and sparkled over our heads and was reflected from the black of the windows; the black-and-white marble floors gave cool contrast; the mirrors in their gilt frames reflected the blues of the delphiniums and Isabelle's palest lavender gown and my pale yellow as we passed and repassed. When we exchanged partners I understood her silence, for Nico was a superbly unobtrusive dancer. He quickly found any idiosyncrasies of his partner, adapted himself, and led with a firm assurance that made dancing a delight. My experience with professional dancers was limited, but I did wonder where he had come by this skill, but then, like Isabelle, just danced for the pleasure of it.

The music shifted to a waltz, we changed partners again, and there appeared Gavin, smoothly guiding Cousin Alexandra. Her flowered chiffon swirled gracefully through their modest whirls, and she was obviously enjoying herself. As they passed us, I heard her say, "I never see you alone. Take me out to the terrace after the next turn."

Amaury was no waltzer, and I stopped him to watch the two. As they twirled to the door we four clapped, quite spontaneously, which pleased Alexandra immensely. She threw us a kiss and sauntered out on Gavin's arm. Amaury started again. I was paying no attention to the murmur coming in my right ear until I heard him say, "You're really prettier than Isabelle, Petra, and much more fun."

I shook my head. Isabelle's superior statuesque beauty was firmly fixed in my mind.

"You are. You've got so much life in your face. Never knew anyone like you." His arm tightened. I pushed him away a little. Isabelle and Nico were unconscious of anything but the music.

"It's hot and I'm tired," I said. "I've had enough."

In a masterful sweep I had not suspected, he whirled me to the door and through and down the terrace until I was quite gasping and ordered him to stop. He did, instantly, but kept my arm, and we went down the steps to the rose garden. He talked a little more about Normandy, and now it was a château he was going to buy when he had money, a small one, but a château. He pressed my arm. "You'd like that, wouldn't you, Petra?"

"Heavens." I managed a giggle of my own ."You need to find an heiress for that, Amaury."

"Oh, I may not. There'll be money, some way. And I'm sure you have enough, anyway, Petra. I don't know what you do, but I have a feeling you've made some money on your own."

This I found distasteful, so I moved away. The scent of roses floated around us, the white gleaming, the red now black in the faint light. A nightingale started to tune up. It was too much, and I was plunged into some nameless sorrow. Before I could savor it, Amaury had seized me and was kissing my hair, my face, my mouth with a rather clumsy fervor. "I'm crazy about you. I've never known anyone like you," he muttered.

Amazed, it took me a moment to raise my hands and break his hold. That surprised him and he looked at me uncertainly. "But you must like me some," he protested.

"Oh, I do. But I don't like being kissed."

"I can make you," and he grabbed me again.

This time I stamped on his foot and jerked my head away. "Amaury. Stop. Don't be silly. How could I feel that way in three days?"

He backed a bit and his eyes seemed to narrow. "Are you laughing at me?"

"Of course not." I was impatient. "I do like you. I always did. But no one could feel as . . . as you seem to wish in such a short time."

He rubbed one hand across his forehead. "I shouldn't

have rushed you. But, all this . . ." His arm swept toward the garden and the moon.

"I know," I sympathized. "It takes us all that way sometimes—roses . . . moon . . . nightingales. . . . Don't worry. We'll forget about it. Let's talk about fertilizers."

"Now you *are* making fun of me. I meant what I said and I will not forget. But I will leave you." He stalked rigidly to the house.

I giggled to myself. Would he interrupt the dance, or go listen to Cousin Eugenia? Perhaps I had been too emphatic. I walked around the garden so as to give him time to get settled and came to the rose arch in the walk.

A tall figure stepped from beneath the roses and took me firmly in its arms. "Since you are so free with your kisses, it is surely my turn," Gavin murmured, and his mouth came down on mine.

It was like nothing that had ever happened to me. The earth sank away beneath my feet and I swayed and was drowning, held by the tenderness and strength of the arms and the kiss to which I gave myself so completely. I could only lie quietly when he raised his head and put his cheek against my hair. "Have you kissed us all like that?" he asked softly.

I was more steady now, and remembered his first words, too. One tactic I had learned early was that when emotion seemed dangerous a quick flip retort would set any man back on his heels and give time for escape from a situation. I had never needed one more than now. "Well, there's still Roger. I can't tell about him," I said as brightly as I could, though I knew my voice shook.

He drew in his breath, and as his arms dropped I stepped back. "Furthermore," and my voice was steady, "if in your snooping you had been close enough to hear what was said those other times you throw at me, you'd have known that I don't like to be kissed, not by anyone."

I ran through the arch and along the terrace. The hall was empty. I could hear Alexandra describing a country weekend to Eugenia. I thought of looking for Amaury and flirting with him madly just so Gavin could see. But that would have no effect and was too much trouble.

So I went straight to the bottles on the side table. I must stop feeling those hard arms holding me so gently, must stop thinking of those few minutes. Tomorrow I would forget, or face what had happened. I refused to let myself stay awake all night, and the Scotch would help. I took a good gulp.

"Petra," began Eugenia acidly, "do you think you should drink—"

"Let her alone," ordered Alexandra. "I have a feeling Petra can cope with anything she decides to drink, or any reason for her to do so."

She smiled warmly, and I moved my lips to smile back. I lit a cigarette and listened without hearing as they reminisced, then went to my room and fell asleep before I had told myself I was a fool more than fifty times.

8

Isabelle said she had a bathing suit, in fact, two, when I found her cutting some roses the next morning, and so had no need to go to Salisbury, but she thanked me nicely for asking. She must have been softening toward me—and perhaps I was toward her—for she held out a handful of roses for me to smell and waved as I left the garden.

I was backing out the Austin when Cousin Alexandra hailed me. "Yoo, hoo, stockings," she yodeled from the door. I went to meet her.

"So glad you're going to Salisbury, dear. I have no stockings left, all torn, with runners, though I don't really see why. At my age stockings are *essential*." Her voice was raised. "Providentially I thought of you. So glad I caught you."

She took my arm and propelled me to the car. She was a little plump, but carried herself so well and had kept her figure so nicely that she was always impressive. She always got her own way. But I was glad to have her company. Nothing could happen with her beside me.

We were through the village and on the main road when I glanced at her again. The arched eyebrows were drawn in a frown.

"I am somewhat perturbed, Petra," she began, "or, if that is too strong a word, I could say, disturbed." She half turned in her seat. "I am telling you, for someone else should know, and I had no chance to tell Gavin.

"There are some phone calls I wish to make to London, private calls. I intended to make them from the phone in the study, since Gavin was not there. I lifted the receiver and asked for a trunk line and distinctly heard another receiver being taken from the hook before I had finished speaking. I waited. I was sure I could hear breathing. When the operator said it would be ten minutes before she had a line I said it did not matter, and I heard the other receiver click very gently. Someone obviously had been listening. I have no car here. Yesterday I told Sloane to drive up to London and pick up some clothes and the mail. I feel I should not wait for his return. So I thought of the ruse of the stockings, and of you. What do you think?"

"I think you're very resourceful," I told her promptly.

"It's those pictures. I did not believe in them even at the beginning when the boys told me about them. But now . . . I wonder what they know. . . ." She brooded briefly, then sat up briskly as we came into town. "Take me to the White Hart and leave me there. Come back in an hour and wait, if I am not ready, in the bar. And, here"—she pulled out a ten-pound note—"get me as many pairs of stockings for this as you can. Here's the size and kind." She produced a long filmy stocking and laid it on the seat.

"It's been cut!" I exclaimed as I glimpsed it dangling.

"Of course," she agreed. "I had to have an excuse. I was in a hurry, but I put proper runs in the others."

I laughed. "You must have read Agatha Christie."

"Naturally. I find Miss Marple most admirable and wish I had her opportunities. And could I make you a present of the new bathing suit?"

I patted her hand. "No, dear, I can take care of that, but thank you." She nodded as though confirmed in some thought.

Again I parked near the cathedral, found the bathing suit and stockings. I hesitated a moment over the suit, for it was my first bikini, but it was my favorite blue and anyway my figure, in its own way, was as good as Isabelle's.

My sherry at the White Hart was almost gone when Alexandra swept from the door behind the bar and ordered a pink gin and another sherry and smiled at the rotund barman. "Mr. Vane let me use his phone in the office," she explained. "So much more convenient." When she paid for the drinks there was an extra folded note for him. As we left town a little later, I noticed a car, a black saloon, drawing out from an alley. There were long scratches on both front fenders, I noticed, and than a lorry came between us.

Alexandra settled herself comfortably. "Did the calls get through?" I asked.

"Quite satisfactorily, thank you. But I may need to come again, if some letters don't arrive quickly enough." She thought for a moment. "I shared one thing with you, Petra. Now I'll share another. At least I know now what the boys know, or think they know."

"Boys?"

"The Montlucs, of course. I had been wondering why they stayed around when the search of the Priory revealed nothing. They must be sure something, somehow, will turn up. You will find," she went off at a tangent, "that one of the few compensations for growing older is that one's friends do also, and some of them rise to positions where they can be useful and do so willingly because of the youth you shared. Though that's hardly true of Michel de Ferlé."

"Who's he?"

"Free French during the war. He stayed on in England, since his home and vineyards were quite destroyed, tramped over by all the armies at one time or another. He's done well in business in London, but he was very active in those first war years and parachuted and came back several times. He was the only one I could think of who might know something about the Princess. He did —he's still a dreadful gossip. It seems some memoirs have been published in France by one of those little men who know great ones and then blow up their own past beyond all recognition when it is safe to write about it. Michel had been sent a copy of the book. The Princess is mentioned in it, all the usual things about her, charm and courage and what everyone knows. But there was also a sentence that said that once, when funds were low, she left town and reappeared with some things she had managed to save from France. She was able to sell them for a good sum which she gave, of course, to the Free French. And she said she had more *things* she could sell later, if necessary. Then she went to France and never returned. That was all Michel himself knew, but he remembered hearing of the incident, though not what the *things* were, and doubts that anyone knows. The boys must have seen the memoir, and that, combined with this discovery that some Montluc pictures are indeed missing, brought them here. Poor thing." She sighed. "A most delightful woman and a genuinely good one. And such a patriot! Everyone adored her." She sighed again. "It does make one wonder, though. There must be others who have seen that blasted book and could find out what happened. Just because we haven't noticed any strangers doesn't mean there may not be some around. Stealing art here and in France seems to have become a profitable occupation for thieves, judging by the accounts in the papers. I wouldn't like the Montluc pictures to be stolen, wherever they are. But I don't believe for a minute they're at the Priory."

She looked out of the window, was reminded of an incident of her youth, and began to entertain me with amusing and usually scandalous tales hung on names I barely remembered. We were nearly at the village when a big black saloon tore by us. It was going so quickly I glanced at it and saw a long scratch on the left front fender.

Roger appeared at three with a large car and a huge tea basket, assuring us there would be a bath house for us to change in and that the water was perfect. His face lighted when Isabelle smiled at him approvingly.

It was nearly an hour's drive to the coast but well worth it. The beach was small and white, the pavilion well equipped, and the water warm in the shallows with just enough tang further out to make swimming fun.

We were all sufficiently expert so that there was no problem. My new bathing suit looked as well on me as I had hoped. Isabelle's lovely figure showed to fine advantage, and I admired it without envy but was glad we were different types. Roger lost some inhibitions in the water and turned playful, and to my surprise Isabelle did not object. The brothers swam extremely well. Afterward, when we lay on the beach, I noticed their backs were smooth and tanned as if they had been much in the sun. We had a long and lazy tea and decided not to return for dinner and had Isabelle phone her mother from the nearest booth. Roger took us further west to an inn he favored, which was quite as good as he claimed it was. Then we decided a visit to the cinema would round off the evening nicely. In Exeter we found of all things an old picture of the Marx Brothers. It was dated, and some of it incomprehensible, but it struck us as hilarious, and we loved it and arrived home very late. Roger had been an expert and unobtrusive host and I thought Isabelle a fool not to grab him.

Some of the day's gaiety lingered the next morning, for when Nico suggested we walk around the grounds to see the places where we used to play, we all agreed cheerfully. I was glad to be kept busy and in company; Mrs. Carrick and her present could wait another day. I did not see how this return to our youth would help in the search because obviously none of us (except me with my silver box) had hidden anything except colored stones or a broken toy, and pictures would not be left in the open, but, I realized, it did keep us all together, so no one could go off alone.

At last I mentioned the ruins of Marden Castle, and

on learning it wasn't a mile away, the boys brightened considerably. How anything could have been hidden there was not clear, but I would enjoy seeing it again, for it was one cause of my abiding affection for ruins.

When we were young it had been only an unsafe, crumbling, square keep, but some enterprising new owner had added a car park, a three-pence charge at a stile, and a railed-in flooring on top of the two-story tower so trippers could admire the view. Inside the thick walls a wooden staircase with a guard rail mounted one side to a lower platform, where a second flight of steps led to the trapdoor and the tower platform. The original stone steps, which I had once used without a thought, were even more crumbling and unsafe, rising along one wall to turn and cross to within a few feet of the small landing. The lancet windows that had been set in the archers' slits still retained some of their tracery. Two hooded fireplaces faced each other from opposite walls, and one gaped above, where once had been the second floor.

Across the dirt floor under the old staircase a flat-arched door led to blackness. Ever resourceful, Nico pulled a pencil flashlight from his breast pocket. Cement steps had replaced the ancient stone slabs leading downward, but the floor blocks of the old guardroom were original and massive. At one side was another fireplace.

"How many fires for a small tower!" Isabelle remarked idly.

"How much wood they had to cut to keep warm in your English winters," said Amaury the farmer, as he picked up a plank from a discarded pile and poked it up the chimney. At about three feet it stuck, bringing down soot and dirt and half a brick. Bending nearly double, he peered inside. "It slants, and there's nothing here," he reported.

Isabelle murmured something about bats as she retreated. I followed her outside. Most of the ivy I had once used for climbing the walls was gone, but two vines still draped themselves picturesquely over an empty window.

She watched me as we strolled around. "You used to come here by yourself and climb, didn't you? I was always jealous of you, you know."

I hooted. "How could you be, Isabelle? You had everything, always, looks, clothes, family, money, a home."

Her cheeks had a faint glow, and short golden strands were blowing around her face. "Yes. I had all that, and they were a help. But you were always so energetic and interested in everything and full of life and could do so much what you wished. You lit up when you were excited. I knew I was insipid in comparison. Though I jeered and called you redhead, which you never really were, I knew your hair and eyes were lovely. I never had your brains, either. I used to wish sometimes we could really be friends. But Mother wouldn't let me, you know. She never wanted me to be nice to you, so I got in the way of being unpleasant to satisfy her. She said I'd get some of your hoydenish ways and kept us apart on purpose and kept away herself. I even envied you that— you didn't have her everlastingly *at* you as I did. I've always had to hide everything from her, but she always gets her own way in the end. She *whines* until she does. Now, being with you again after all this time, and the four of us having fun together, I can't help looking back and being sorry for all I missed with you when we were children.''

That was a long speech for Isabelle and explained a good deal, but before I could think of what to say, the two men were coming out of the tower. The flush deepened on her cheeks as she turned to them. Could it be that the aloof Isabelle had fallen at last? Nico, of course. Perhaps this time Eugenia wouldn't get her own way, but I wondered what Isabelle would get.

It turned gray after lunch. Gavin was off on farm business. Eugenia and Alexandra went calling by themselves. We tried a little bridge but soon lost interest. When I went for another pack of cigarettes I found I was out. Sometimes extra packs were kept in the pantry, so I went to ask Manson, but there were none. I said I'd run down for a supply.

At the village I bought the Picadillys from Mrs. Parrett and, seeing on the counter a motor map of the county, added that on the chance some of the roads might have been changed. The lanes wound around the quadrangle of the Priory lands and across some farms in a bewildering tangle, but most of them seemed to have stayed in place.

I was on the straight of the little road behind the beech woods when I noticed the car behind me. I was going slowly, but since the road was humpbacked and narrow, with a shallow grass-covered dip between tarmac and hedgerows, I slowed still further and pulled to the left edge so any car would have had room to pass. The other car came on so slowly that I glanced in the mirror; it was black, with scratches on the fender, and it was coming straight at me. I edged over further and opened my mouth to shout when the black car moved past and the rear fender clipped my front just enough to spin the Austin around. I tugged at the wheel and cut the engine. It was frightening. My hands were shaking, and the Austin sat squarely across the road. It had been deliberate; the driver had known just what he wished to do.

The other car had swung off the road and parked. A man with a cloth cap pulled down almost to his eyes got out and came back to me as I sat waiting for my breathing to settle down.

"You was too near the center, miss," he said, touching his cap.

"I wasn't," I protested shakily. "You did that on purpose."

"Right, miss." He opened the door and got in beside me. "I did. We're going to have a little talk, and I couldn't think of no other way to get you off by yourself. Just drive on quiet now and take the next lane to the right."

"I'm going back to the house." I controlled my voice. "Get out of my car."

"Not yet, I won't. Drive on nicely now." He looked down at his right hand as he swiveled in the seat to face me and I followed his glance. A short black revolver was pointing at me.

"You wouldn't use it!"

"Not to shoot. But it can give you a tap on the head, and then you might have a real accident. But all I want to do is talk. Drive on now."

His English was certainly colloquial, but there was a faint foreign tone in his voice. He was so matter-of-fact I believed him, and pressed the starter. What in heaven's name could this thug have to say to me? I drove on, turned as he directed, and we ended on a disused track beyond a copse. Here he turned off the car switch and pocketed the key. I started to open my door, but a hand came down on my arm in a grip that hurt, and hurt more as he found and pressed a muscle.

"Just wait now. You can go in a minute. I want to help you."

"Help?"

"You don't understand, do you? Said so all along. Look. Everyone says you know something about these missing pictures. If you and me worked together we wouldn't have to split with others. You get the pictures. I'll take them to London. Or"—expansively—"you could come up with me, if you don't trust me. That way we get it all, just us two."

I settled back in my seat. Perhaps here was some sort of a clue. "Why does everyone think I know about missing pictures?" I asked with round-eyed innocence.

"Stands to reason. You were here. You'll have to tell, sooner or later."

"But I don't know anything," I protested.

"Holding out for more of a split, eh?" The round, nondescript face above the dark suit grew ugly as the black eyes narrowed. "You're a fool if you do. That's what comes of amateurs. I can tell you you won't get anything. The yellow-haired young gentleman, if you're thinking of him, you might work it; he's trustful. But the one they call Nico . . . he's been in the game too long. He's tough. You'll be lucky if you don't get a knife in the back when he's done."

"How do you know?" I tried to ask casually.

"Because . . ." he began and stopped. "Come on, now. Fifty-fifty's fair. If you can't get them alone, let me in tonight, and I'll get them and we'll be off."

When he had turned to face me, there had been something familiar about the way the head was set on the shoulders. Of course . . . the man with his back to the window in Cousin Aylmer's study! "You've tried this trick already," I said. "Only you and whoever was with you didn't find anything—that time I was knocked out."

"Right," he agreed. "That's why I've come to you. Sensible for us both."

"And if I came with you, I'd get disposed of before we ever reached London."

"If you don't trust me . . ." he began sullenly.

"Of course I don't. And, anyway, I don't know anything, as I keep saying."

He stared at me venomously. "Playing it that way, are you? Then you'll get no help from me when the cards are down. But if you change your mind, I'm in the caravan on the lane. But don't try to get away, for I'll be watching."

Before I could think of a crushing answer, he leaned across and opened my door and shoved me out on the ground. "You can walk back. But I'll leave your car where you ran into me. Think on what I've been saying. And you better watch out for yourself."

He backed my car expertly to the lane and I heard it move away swiftly.

Furious at him, and at myself for letting myself be kidnapped that way, I got up and brushed my skirt. Where was I? Those lanes, the track and copse . . . I was in back of the Williams farm, and there should be a path through the fields and woods to the lane behind the Priory. The cigarettes were still in the car, which added to my fury, and I stalked over the ruts, deciding what to say when I went to the caravan to give him a piece of my mind.

But the more I walked the more I cooled down. This was not the sort of man you could tell off. There had been an air of matter-of-fact violence about him, and menace hung over all he implied. His assurance about me was uncomfortable. I had to admit I had seen more of the Princess than anyone. I thought back over my times with her and became more convinced than ever that there had been no hint she had deposited anything of value at the Priory. I certainly could honestly tell myself, and anyone, that I knew nothing. But I was shaken. I had thought I could always take care of myself. Confronted by this tangle of unbelief and threats, I was not so sure.

The path through the field was rough going, and by the time I reached the woods I was shaking with reaction. But I tramped ahead. I must get to the car—I believed he would leave it as he said—and back to the house, though I was not sure why. But the woods were green and soothing, and by the time I reached the lane the urgency had left me and I sat down on a stone. I would rest before walking the last mile.

The grass by the lane covered the sound of hoofbeats, and Gavin and Black Peter were almost on me before I heard them. He swung down and knelt beside me. "Petra! What's happened? A man went by in your car. I followed and found it parked and he's vanished. I came looking for you."

He was so friendly, so concerned, the Gavin I had found over the tea at the inn, that I told him the truth. "I was kidnapped. Oh, not for long. A stranger made me drive away and wanted me to find the pictures for him and then we'd divide the swag together. When I wouldn't agree, he pushed me out of the car and drove away."

The tanned face closed down, the gray eyes were no longer friendly. "That's incredible," he drawled. "No one will believe you."

"I wouldn't think of telling anyone else."

"I'm duly flattered. But it's as poor a story as saying you were hit in the study that morning. There was no one in the house; I searched again, and no sign of a car. You're bright enough to do better. Here, I'll take you back to the car and you can think up a new version."

He rose and helped me to my feet, and I waited wearily while he brought over Black Peter and lifted me to the saddle and mounted behind. It was not very comfortable, sitting with my legs dangling down, and I wondered how the ladies used to be graceful about it when they were abducted—and by knights in armor at that. The only thing to do was relax against the firm chest, and I did, with a sigh. An arm went around me gently, and his head bent.

"What's it all about, Petra? I ask you again. Can't you tell me? I'd like to be friends, as we were that afternoon. I said then I'd like to help. I meant it."

That afternoon had been fun. I looked up into the steady eyes beneath the thick lashes and brows. There were faint lines at the corners I had not noticed before.

Return to Aylforth *128*

Weather or laughter? It was a good forehead, too, and the dark hair had enough curl to keep from lying flat. Dreamily I lifted one finger and touched the scar that broke the right eyebrow. "How did that happen?" I asked.

"A drunken Cree decided he didn't like my face and tried to improve it drastically. I hit him harder but not quite soon enough. And that's the truth."

At the word *truth* I tried to sit up, but the arm held me in place. I relaxed, perforce. It was not so uncomfortable after all, riding this way. I no longer wondered so many elopements on horseback had been successful.

"I don't understand you," I murmured. "Don't you ever trust anyone?"

"Plenty of men."

"But not women?" I pursued.

"Oh," his tone lightened. "I learned not to do that long ago, when Gladys in the fourth grade abandoned me for a boy who could both do her homework and give her rides on a scooter."

"That's hardly a good excuse, now."

"There was another girl, later, of course. But she found a businessman who could give her the bright lights of Montreal as an engineering student working for a degree couldn't." He still kept it light.

"Even she's no reason for never believing me."

"No. I agree. But don't you see it's mostly your own fault? I keep finding you in such strange situations. . . . And all this talk about what you might know and won't tell . . . I wish you would clear it all up for me."

"I can't." Only later did I realize that sounded ambiguous too. "But there's more. You didn't believe me that first afternoon by the ruin."

"I didn't. Even though I'd seen you talking to a strange man, I thought you were just a trespassing tripper. I should have known better, and I apologize. I only realized who you might be as you walked away. I began to wonder . . ."

"Why?"

He continued reluctantly. "I had heard of you. In talking about the memorial service, Isabelle asked if Perdita should be told. Eugenia snapped her head off, said there was no need to tell anyone, that Perdita had always been independent and ungrateful, a chit, in short, and would only come back to Aylforth if there were something she wanted. Isabelle started to protest but collapsed when her mother glared. I suppose those words stayed in the back of my mind. Now I know she spoke unfairly and from malice, but I'm still wondering about you."

This time I did stiffen. We were at the car, anyway. "You quoted her as saying I was fanciful. I've always believed friends took each other on trust. Obviously you don't wish to be a friend, or you wouldn't blow hot and cold about me as you do."

I began to try to slide down from the saddle. He caught and held me tightly. "Of course I blow hot and cold." His eyes were bright and angry. "I waste too much time just trying to figure you out. Don't you know half of me wants to believe you, trust you, and half can't?"

I put my fists against his chest and pushed. "Then you'll just have to let the two halves fight it out, won't you?" I was sweet about it. "Help me down, please."

He did, instantly, but my knees were shaking again, and he had to help me to the car. There was no sign of the man, of course, but the new road map lay on the seat. His brows drew together as he noticed the yellow oblong. "I'm surprised you have that, since you know the country so well. Or is this for someone else? For a rendezvous? What *did* happen about the car? Tell me the truth, Petra."

"I have," I said firmly.

"Then which one are you working with? You're the focus of all this strange attention; there must be some reason. Is it Nico, whom you met secretly in the lane? Is it Amaury, who can't leave you a moment? Is it this man you say abducted you? Who is the source of assault and battery? Or is it someone else yet for whom you go prying and looking?"

"There's no one." I was angry at last. I'd had enough questions for the afternoon. "Leave me alone."

"I don't believe you." He gave me a little shake. "What is it that makes these people so sure something is hidden at the Priory?"

"It must be that book, and the letter too, probably, and they're all wrong about me. I don't know a thing about any bloody pictures." Until that moment I had forgotten about the letter Nanny had told me about, and I was past thinking.

"Letter?" He went back a pace. "Then you *are* in league with them—or on your own." His eyes narrowed. "You could only have learned about the letter from one of them. Thetwin wouldn't tell you. He's honor itself. He found it between the pages of some old farm estimates in the wall safe, showed it to me, and I told him to send it to the Count at Montmézay, unopened. Did you meet Nico, or Amaury, in Paris and arrange the visit? What did the letter say?"

I was surprised out of my anger. "I don't know."

"So they're secretive too, perhaps. When did you learn about the letter?"

"Nanny told me. Long ago."

"A likely story! On a par with your others."

There was no use trying to convince him. "I can't help if you don't believe me." I opened the car door.

He stopped me, his touch and voice gentle again. "I want to help you, Petra. But you refuse to let me. How do I know what to think or feel?"

"It's nothing to me what you think or feel." I got in the car, and he stepped back.

"Very well. Go ahead and work by yourself, if you are. But don't come to me for help."

"Don't worry. I won't." I managed a smile. The car jerked to a start. As I careened along the lane, I could see in the mirror that he watched me out of sight.

9

Later, while dressing, I let myself think about Gavin. But what could I think? I was sure it was not his nature not to know his own mind and that he was as annoyed at himself as at me. Wasted time thinking about me, he'd said. Served him right, and I smiled into my mirror. But I had to admit I didn't know how I felt about him, either, except that he was formidably attractive and could be nice one minute and infuriating the next. Well, if he could wait to make up his mind I could too, and laugh at myself while I waited. So, it was another embarrassing encounter we would both ignore. But there was also the man from the black car and his threats and warnings. It was all preposterous, of course. I'd ignore everything and mind my own business.

The air was more sultry and heavy after dinner. Over the bridge game Eugenia complained and Alexandra almost snapped. We stopped thankfully by ten. No one suggested a walk outside except Nico, who took Isabelle up and down the terrace, and they came in when we started upstairs.

It was several hours before the storm broke with a crash that jerked me upright in bed. A sheet of lightning showed a sudden crystal curtain of rain that became a mad flood of water. I went to close the window, for the wind could veer in any direction. As I fastened the latch, I saw in my mind another window that was still open, the one in the attic I had used for escape over the roof. Gavin and I had been so occupied arguing, when we returned there, we had forgotten it, I was sure. Water would flood in, and though there was nothing that could be hurt, it would do the floor and ceiling below no good. Since I had opened it in the first place, I had better go close it. Slippers—negligée—torch. I paused. This was one private time I could finish going through Nanny's trunk. There was always someone around during daylight. I retrieved the key from my blouse pocket and opened my door carefully. The storm might waken people, but the rain was rattling on the roof like a drum corps gone mad, and the thunder was marching around us in circles. Smaller sounds would be hidden.

The bolt was on at the attic door; again I bolted it from the inside. As I reached the top of the stairs, another sheet of lightning showed the window wide open and the floor glistening beneath it. I pushed the window shut against the gusty wind and carried two of the chairs with broken backs over beside the trunk and propped the torch on one. Carefully I lifted out each garment and laid it on the chair. Beneath the old bathrobe were some dresses, slips, nightgowns that needed mending, all obviously Nanny's, a tweed coat and a black winter one for best, a quilt, handmade, and a green crocheted afghan. Next were the clothes the Princess had left, a soft blue wool Chanel *tailleur*, a rose-colored chiffon dinner dress, blouses and summer dresses. I was glad I could dump the problem of what to do with them on Alexandra. Then came a new wool bathrobe, the one I was to take, and beneath lay the battered brown leather top of an old valise, fitting in neatly, with space to spare. Yes, Nanny had said she had put the one she had brought from France in the trunk.

The valise was unlocked. Here were a few more of Nanny's clothes, older than the others. The canvas lining was too near the top; it might guard still more of Nanny's thrifty hoardings beneath it.

The lining was tucked in around some flat objects wrapped in linen pillowcases. I undid the nearest and was looking at a charming young girl in a white dress poised against an arbor of roses. I lifted it out and held up the torch. The canvas had been cut from the frame. The next package held its mate, a young man in court dress. My hands were shaking as I searched for a signature. In the corner I found "A. Watteau." I was so frightened I put out the torch for a moment. Oh, the clever Princess. She had trusted no one would bother with the suitcase of the nurse. The space was not half full; the *things* she had sold for the Free French had come from this suitcase. She must have left these others for future need.

The next pillowcase enclosed a Van Gogh, a green, sunny field with poppies and cypresses. It was almost defiantly gay, with one little white cloud in the sky. Somewhere I had seen a reproduction of a larger, similar picture. Next was a Chardin still life, and though the fruit glowed, it said nothing to me. The last picture was longer, a Monet, perhaps a study for his series of the banks of the Seine. The blue water rippled as it reflected the sky, and the gray-green trees bent a little in the wind. At once I felt this was the one I loved above them all. But I mustn't feel—here and now. I must put them back and think later.

Pictures, rewrapped, went back in place beneath the lining, Nanny's clothes on top, the valise clasped, the other clothes covering that, and the trunk locked again, chairs replaced. I scurried from the attic, bolted the door, and tiptoed to my room. The rain was still pounding, but the thunder had moved across the hills. At the knob of my door my fingers found something alien. My torch showed a thin black string dangling from the handle, the other end hanging from a tack on the frame. Someone wanted to know if I left my room! Had he already come by to check? If he hadn't, I'd give him a turn when he did. I pulled loose the string and the tack and stored both in my suitcase, then returned to bed.

Admiration for the Princess blotted out thought. Once she had been my dear companion whom I wistfully hoped to emulate. Now I must respect her resourcefulness and her courage. Something must have frightened her about London, perhaps everything had, brave as she was. She had told Nanny she had no one she could trust but Cousin Aylmer . . . She must have thought she was taking all sensible precautions—leaving the pictures safely in the country away from bombs and thieves, the note for Cousin Aylmer (what *had* it said?) to be explained by herself, or Maxim, or someone she could trust. Now the paintings belonged to Amaury and Nico, with certainly a share from the Chardin, at least, for the uncle and the school.

Amaury and Nico . . . I was reluctant to face that combination. Amaury was genuine, I was sure; although he had not shown that temper Nanny had deplored, he remembered things, and that knowledge of, and enthusiasm for, farming could not be faked. But he was guileless and trusting toward his brother. He had promised to share everything he learned. I wished I had heard more through the closet wall, but every time I had tried, the door of the other closet had been closed and the muffled words quite indistinguishable.

Nico, now, was something else again. That conversation I *had* heard took on more meaning. Nico had sounded professional. I did not trust him—more than that, I was suspicious of him. He had threatened me, to my face and behind my back . . . he had mentioned some power behind him. "Organization," and "We do not make mistakes," and "Markets." That man in the car had said he was tough and experienced. Manson was working with him. Amaury would turn the pictures, if I gave them to him, over to Nico, and he and Manson and the other man would decamp with them. As well as Alexandra, I had read accounts of art thefts. If I brought out these paintings, somehow they would be taken away forever.

But what should I do? What would the Princess wish me to do? See they got to the rightful owners, of course. How? Perhaps, given a little more time, Nico would betray his true intentions, so Amaury could have no doubts and would take over. Or perhaps there would be some proof my own doubts were wrong. I was not used

. . . . 137

to feeling so uncertain and inadequate. But I owed it to my friend the Princess to see her legacy went where she would wish—insofar as I could.

One thing was clear to me. I now had a duty and a mission. I could not leave Aylforth until the future of the paintings was settled, and in the right way. No matter what ambiguous threats had been thrown at me, or said about me, or what unknown danger might be hovering ahead, here I must stay.

But I needed wise advice. Gavin? And see his mouth tighten as he did not say, "I knew it," and the scorn in his eyes for a liar? Never. Cousin Alexandra, with her worldly good sense, would advise me to have them carried to London for safekeeping while the Count was informed. But there would be that period while they were in the house, and who knew if they would get safely to the city, or even to Salisbury, no matter how we tried to keep it all secret? Mr. Thetwin? There was an idea. Best of them all, he could tell me what to do. Perhaps I could shake the man in the black car. Or even if he tried to frighten me again, I could make it, somehow. And I'd have to hide the pictures in a safer place until I had a chance to go to Salisbury. The trunk could be pried open: someone would think of it soon. But what place was safe?

Next morning I was more convinced than ever that I must talk with Mr. Thetwin. I went and sat in the sun on the terrace so I would be conspicuously idle while I thought of ways and means. Over to the left came the clip, clip of a gardener trimming the yew. A boy began to cut the lawn unenthusiastically. Swifts chased each other above the oaks, and a robin was pleased enough with himself to tell the world all was well.

Gavin strolled around a corner and sat down beside me. "Now what are you plotting?" he asked pleasantly enough, as if nothing had been said in the back lane. "When I see you quiet, like this, I'm sure you're planning something unusual damn mean, as they used to say in *Stalky & Co.*, in case you can't place that as a quotation."

"Thank you," I said gently. "I place it. In fact, I know my Kipling quite well." I ignored the first question.

"You do?" He looked surprised and pleased. "He gave me my enthusiasm for England. Unusual in the female young in this age to know more than the *Just So Stories*."

"Which I always took to heart," I countered swiftly, "both the elephant's child and the cat who walked by herself were my favorite characters."

"Obviously. And their influence is still upon you."

I had laid myself open to that. "I could match you quote for quote, including the poems," I offered to change the line of thought.

> "They shut the road through the woods
>   Seventy years ago,"

he began softly.

> "Wind and rain have undone it again,
>   And now you would never know
>   That there was once a road through the woods,"

I continued as softly.

He came out of that mood quickly. "We'll have a fine time capping each other some rainy afternoon," he promised cordially. "But now, won't you get sunburned out here, or doesn't your skin burn?"

"I may get a few more freckles, but usually I just tan a little. I've never been for a long time in really hot sun, so I don't know about burning," I was surprised enough to answer.

"What do you do in London, anyway?" He watched a butterfly search for honey around one of the urns.

"Oh, I work," I told him vaguely. But I was pleased he asked, and then told myself it was just another way of trying to check up on me. "I like London, but at the moment this is better."

"Yes." He rose smoothly, as controlled as Nico in his movements. "And I mean to keep it better, so I must go see Beckham. Keep out of mischief, Petra, and don't go climbing around any more roofs." Surprisingly, his hand touched my hair, and he was striding into the house. Here was his ambivalent attitude again. What was mine to him? I left that unanswered.

I basked a little more, enjoying the sun and savoring the conversation and wondering if we would find other things we liked together besides Kipling, if we ever should reach open friendship. I decided there were, and I hoped I wouldn't have to climb around on any more roofs. Ruins and castles were more fun. Castles? Then I realized I knew one place where I could hide the paintings. But there were some things I would need. I began to list them to myself. Only Salisbury would have the lot. So I was back to figuring how to get there without being followed, for I could go to the shops after seeing Mr. Thetwin. I'd telephone for an appointment right now.

I couldn't use the phone in the pantry. Cousin Aylmer's study? I slowed down. But did I want to use any phone at all from this house, even for such an innocent-seeming request? Anyone could listen anywhere, as Cousin Alexandra had discovered. I halted in the hall. Suppose I simply walked to the village?

Low angry voices floated out of the study. "I'll do what I please." That was Amaury.

"You'll do what I say and like it. I know what I'm doing. You'll take *my* orders." That was Nico, in a voice of flat menace.

"Why should I?" Amaury was surprised. "I never have and I won't now."

Nico flung out the door and almost ran down the hall to the door at the back. Amaury was grinning as he came out and saw me. "Hello there, Peter. Did you see Nico just now?"

"He went out."

A large shapely hand, but rather too broad, I thought, slipped inside my arm, and the broad tanned face that looked so Nordic smiled down at me. "Let's go after him. We were having a bit of a dust-up just now. But you know Nico. He can't stay mad five minutes."

Well, I couldn't phone now, and I was no longer anxious to, so we strolled out to the brick path that circled the stableyard and vegetable and fruit gardens and led to the back lane. Giggling, we admired the neatness of the gardens and wondered if we dared invade in search of strawberries and decided we didn't and strolled on. There was no sign of Nico until we were through the belt of woods and near the lane. Then we could see him talking to a dark figure nearly hidden by the hawthorn hedgerow. He heard us, made an angry gesture, and the figure was no longer there.

He came striding toward us. "How dare you follow me?" His anger was held down except for his eyes.

"Oh, come off it," Amaury drawled. "We weren't following you." Oh, no? I asked myself and looked at him. His pale-blue eyes were intense, but he was smiling. "Who's your friend?"

"A man passing. But understand here and now you're not to sneak around after me, and you're to do as I say."

"Since when? You're the one who used to take orders. Remember?"

"I never took orders from you." Nico's eyes narrowed. "Do your own remembering, and what I told you to do."

Amaury's eyes widened. "Never?" he asked incredulously. Then he shrugged. "You're being stupid. I'm just surprised you're still mad."

"I usually stay mad quite a long time. And don't call me stupid. Look in your own mirror for a dolt." I almost thought Nico would jump at him, but by a visible effort he relaxed and shrugged in turn. "Let's not have a family quarrel in front of Petra."

"Oh, Peter." Amaury drew my arm a little closer, and his voice lightened. "Peter's one of the family, aren't you? She knows us from long ago. Remember how she used to watch us at first from behind furniture and curtains? Though that didn't last long. Then she was thinking up as much mischief as we were."

Nico bent a winning smile at me, and I knew he did not remember at all. There was no answering reminiscent gleam, and the smile was a quick mask. "Let's get Isabelle and go find some mischief of our own."

"Sure. But she wasn't around then." Amaury's tone was amiable as we turned back to the house. I gabbled something about our stealing strawberries and prized peaches and at the door fled to find her.

But I turned into the downstairs lavatory and splashed cold water on my face. For now I knew something else, and every instinct told me it was dangerous knowledge. I could hear Nanny saying, "Shocking temper that Amaury had. Always ordering his brother around, though Nicholas was older . . . Nicholas never could stay angry no matter what . . . you remember the time Amaury pushed him down on the upturned hoe . . . ten stitches it took."

Nico hadn't remembered so many things he should, always following Amaury's lead when it came to reminiscing. The *Just-So Stories,* the one about the leopard's spots, came back to me. This man *looked* like Nico, but who, even a brother, would notice slight differences after ten years? It had been almost twenty years since the rest of us had seen the boys. He *sounded* like Nico, except when he forgot. But there had been no sign of a scar on his right shoulder as he lay on the sand. His back was as smooth as Amaury's. He was *not* the real Nico.

Looking back at me from the mirror was a white face with wide, frightened eyes. I couldn't go out with that expression. Once, for a short season, I had had a series of bit parts in an experimental theater in the West End. I found I wasn't good enough to stick with acting. But if I ever had learned to master my face I must use that experience now. One way was to put out of my mind this minute all that the discovery implied. I went to find Isabelle, and those minutes helped.

The four of us were in the hall, deciding nothing, when Manson approached me austerely. "Telephone, Miss Norreys. At least I believe it must be you the gentleman desires."

At first my heart sank when I heard the light, cheerful voice, but then it rose. Here was help if I used it properly.

"What does that man mean, he never heard of Miss Peter Norreys? It was hard enough finding you at all until I remembered you'd mentioned a Cousin Aylmer and a piece in the paper about the memorial service. You shouldn't go vanishing on your friends this way, Peter."

I'd almost forgotten I was usually "Peter" in London. He was rushing on.

"I'm practically next door, or at least not far away, and I must see you. Have some good news. Is there some pub where you could meet me for some black bread and watered beer?"

No; it was better for him to come here, open and aboveboard, instead of creeping away to some pub and making everyone wonder what I was doing now. And if he came here, it would be only natural for us to go driving. Mrs. Mellowfield could always stretch any meal.

"You come here for lunch," I told him. "There'll be plenty. There are other people, too, who might interest you."

He made no pretense. "That was what I was hoping you would say, sweet. I have no stomach, really, for black bread. When?"

Return to Aylforth *144*

"Come along now from wherever you are; we'll have time for a cocktail."

"So happy to find civilization amid the forests and byres. If I can also find my way among all the Aylforths, Upper Aylforth, Aylforth Common, and Aylforth-on-the-Dew, I'll be with you. You're quite sure yours is Aylforth Priory? Right. Hold back the cocktails. I won't be lost long."

As he rang off, I heard a receiver click, just as Alexandra had, before I hung up.

Mrs. Mellowfield was most agreeable. Wasn't it lucky she had bought a little extra sole that morning, and Ned could pick some more peas, and she had been thinking of a trifle—but with a guest it should be a soufflé, now, shouldn't it?—and rolls would be no trouble. So I went to find Cousin Eugenia, who was in the upstairs sitting room complaining to Susan about a sheet torn in the laundry. I tried to look at her differently, with Alexandra's words in mind. It didn't work very well, but perhaps, if I kept at it, I might see her as anxious rather than hostile and unkind.

"Could I have a guest for luncheon?" I began, knowing that was too abrupt and I should have made more of a ceremony of the request and first said something about the weather.

She frowned at me. "Really, Pérdita, that is most thoughtless. Mrs. Mellowfield has quite enough to do, and in view of the circumstances . . ." She trailed away uncertainly. "Who is it?"

"Charles Pelham, a friend from London. He's just a few miles away. I couldn't let him think we were inhospitable. We never used to be."

She brightened a little at the thought of another man to see Isabelle, but not much, since he was a friend of mine and therefore dubious, and agreed—if Mrs. Mellowfield was *quite* sure it was no trouble—and went back to poor Susan and the sheet.

On the stairs I met Cousin Alexandra and told her of the guest. She beamed. "Someone from your mysterious past, eh? Quite right, of course, to ask him. Eugenia won't like it. You better tell Gavin; after all he *is* the host."

The other three I found looking at the soggy grass court. They were all surprised I had a friend coming, and I could practically see the men, behind blank faces, turning over the idea and examining what his arrival might mean. Isabelle opened her mouth and I almost felt she was about to say, "But I didn't know you had friends" (I could often read her mind), but she closed it in time and appeared delighted. When Nico draped a casual arm across her shoulders and said, "Good-o. Couldn't play anyway," she blushed and moved a shade closer. I began to feel sorry for her and switched my thoughts and grinned brightly at them all.

For Charles I changed into a new pink linen and then found Gavin in the study. He noticed the dress, I could tell, but when I announced that company was coming, he looked down at the desk. "Always delighted to have your friends, of course," he murmured. So I left him.

10

Wheels of his red Bentley spurting gravel, Charles arrived with a flourish. He was dressed in country tweeds, so I knew he was off somewhere on a long weekend. Though a good five feet ten, he looked short beside the others. I knew him well and that the bright brown eyes in the blandly innocent round face saw everything. He waited at the open door until Manson had arranged the tray for cocktails, caught my eye and nodded approvingly. This was just the sort of house and service he liked. Exuberantly he bussed me on both cheeks before I could introduce him formally, when he became his most suave. The bussing was a little out of his role, but I never objected to his infrequent kiss for we both knew it was all in the line of business. He took a very dry martini and settled by Alexandra, for he loved Edwardian ladies and got along with them famously. The two beamed at each other as they fenced, each trying to find out more information than was imparted.

He let her win the first round. Yes, he was on his way west, to near Totnes, and he did know the Luttrells. But then he asked who everyone at Aylforth was and, thwarted, she had to tell him. At the end he made the telling point that the country air was much to be preferred to that of London. Amaury was watching him amusedly. Nico was talking to Isabelle in a corner, and from her complete absorption I knew she was not hearing a word. Gavin appeared fascinated by the trees he saw through the windows, and Eugenia was fidgeting. I had decided to break up the fencing match when luncheon was announced.

Over the sole the skirmishing began again with, "What do you do in London, Mr. Pelham?" from Alexandra.

Charles flashed a glance at me and stepped in boldly. "I am a literary agent, Lady Harborne," he told her with an air.

It caught them all off guard, particularly Eugenia, who said what they were thinking. "How odd that Pérdita should know you!"

"What?" He looked at the astonished faces and laughed delightedly. "Score one for me, Peter. Your name is given away at last. She never would admit what the *P* stood for, you know, and persisted in P. professionally, or Peter or Petra as a concession."

I couldn't be annoyed, so I laughed with him. "I never did care for that fancy of my mother's, so I just did the best I could with it."

"We've always called her Petra because she fussed so about Pérdita. She made the name herself when she was small," explained Eugenia in a tone that disclaimed all responsibility.

"But *we* called her Prickly Peter when we were young," put in Amaury brightly.

Eugenia always had a single-track mind. "But how . . . ?" she began again.

Charles looked around the table in amazement. Gavin, I could tell, was withdrawn to at least a mile from all the goings-on, though he smiled at the right places. I knew what was coming and half regretted it, though I should have realized it would be inevitable with Charles on the scene.

"My dear, you mean to say they don't know? I can't understand why someone hasn't recognized the name, or, for that matter, why you haven't told them."

"There seemed no point."

"It's too good to keep. Your Perdita"—and he cocked his head on one side as he watched Alexandra and Gavin —"is P. Norreys, a successful short-story writer and playwright, with one show on last season, and still running, and another just opened to plaudits. She's been wearing herself out all spring with rewriting and rehearsals. Both plays, as you don't know, are mystery-comedies. She's one of the few who have moved from short stories and a little acting to doing plays. And I'm lucky to be her agent."

I knew they'd have been more impressed if I had become a golf champion, won blue ribbons at a horse show, or sued a duke for breach of promise. Still, they looked surprised. I dropped my eyes modestly to the soufflé, after a side glance at Gavin. Without moving a muscle he had become alert.

"P. Norreys," he said softly. "Mystery-comedy. Short

stories, even in Canadian magazines. I might have known. You're good at stories."

Somehow that took away some of the pleasure from Alexandra's "Petra! I'm proud of you."

"Cousin Aylmer always said you were the clever one," Isabelle pointed out. "It must have been all those mystery novels in his study that gave you the notion to write some on your own."

I had never thought to trace my devotion to tales of mystery, but she was probably right. The polite murmurs from the Montlucs showed the name meant nothing to them.

Charles was satisfied with his bomb. He winked at me and finished his soufflé and gave it an accolade by taking a second helping. He was smug as he began to answer Alexandra's questions about my plays.

We all strolled out to the terrace after coffee. Gavin shook hands heartily with Charles. "So glad you came, Mr. Pelham. Get Petra to show you around the house, the grounds, the countryside—she knows it well." He nodded somewhere over Charles's shoulder and strode away to Charles's "So good of you to have me, sir."

I was thankful Gavin had made the suggestion for me. "Why don't I show you around?" I asked swiftly. "You like old houses."

"Of course, Peter. What do you have, a banqueting hall and a yew alley?" He was a touch condescending, so I knew he must be going to some larger place.

"We'll do the banqueting hall first," I announced and smiled at the others, which stopped any offer to accompany us, and led him away after punctilious farewells and an invitation from Alexandra to come for cocktails when she was back in London.

He liked the hall, and I was tempted to show him the secret room, but someone might come along at the wrong moment. In the center of the hall, where no one could hear, I asked him point-blank if he would drive me on an errand to Salisbury, promising it wouldn't take long. He agreed, charmingly, and I left him to wash up while I went for my purse. The terrace was empty when we returned and I was sorry, for we roared away in style in the Bentley.

I knew Charles was awash with questions but forestalled him by asking his news. I had to decide how much to tell him. It turned out he had made a pleasant sale of rights to my first play through his American agent. "I let him have the rights, on a split commission, of course, just to see what he'd do with them. He's found a good producer who has a director and stars practically lined up already. I know you're pleased, so don't thank me, except for being so bright. Now, tell me about this fascinating collection of characters you have swirling around you."

"Alexandra told you all that, and why we're here."

"True, but that's not enough. There must be more. And what's bothering you, dear? I miss your enthusiasms and all the gay quips. Yes, and you don't look up to snuff. Tell Charles. There's some hanky-panky going on at the Priory?"

"Yes, there is." I could admit that much. But I couldn't involve him in my problems, particularly while he was on some anticipated visit. "But I don't quite know what, at least not enough to explain anything."

. . . . *151*

"Is the new laird involved? He wasn't happy with me."

I hoped I was not blushing. "No," I said too promptly, for he glanced at me. "It's the others, I think. The fox hasn't broken cover."

"He will before long. And if I'm not mistaken, there's a black sedan following us. Know anything about it?"

"Not really. But it has before."

He whistled. "Tell me where to leave you, and I'll lead him away, if that's the game." The spire was rising ahead of us. "I'll park at the White Hart and go to that bookstore nearby and ask about all my authors. Useful research." He grinned, his head on one side to watch me and the rear mirror. "Meet you in an hour." He swung down St. John's Street and was off almost before I was out of the car. I hastened into the hotel and watched a black car with scratches follow the red.

At Mr. Thetwin's the elderly secretary shook his head mournfully. Mr. Thetwin had been in an accident, struck by a car while driving home. Nothing serious, but his ankle was broken, and he would be in the hospital two days more at least. No visitors now. But once he was home he could see me, of course. So my hope was gone—temporarily, anyway.

In case the black car began cruising around the streets trying to pick us up, I started evasive action. There was an alley that led to a car park facing a back entrance to a Woolworth's. The ironmonger was opposite Woolworth's and would surely have a back door. At Woolworth's I bought some more batteries for my torch, some large sheets of heavy plastic, a large black carryall such as Nanny once had, and some good stout cord. At the ironmonger's I found two different weights of rope and a master key that would fit old-fashioned door locks such as those at the Priory. I could think of nothing else and found my way to the car, where Charles was reading a flashy novel such as he would never sell himself. He eyed my large brown-paper-covered parcel.

"Put it on the floor where it won't show. Now I'll take you back, but try to find some ducky little lanes that twist. That black car did follow me until I was nearly here."

He claimed he was both lost and dizzy from twisting before he pulled into the back lane and stopped the car. As I began to thank him, he dropped an arm around my shoulder. "I can't help the nagging thought that something unpleasant is going on here that might mean trouble, even danger, for you, Peter. And that thought has suddenly made me realize something—and I've been watching you. You're different here from in London somehow, softer perhaps. Or perhaps someone's been making love to you? That brings out the best in a girl."

I squirmed around a little in the seat to look at him. He had quite a different expression himself, though he had always been kind, amusedly concerned, and genuinely helpful over the Ted debacle. Suddenly he leaned over and kissed me, nicely and gently, on my lips. My mouth must have fallen open, for he smiled and patted me.

"Don't look so astonished. We've been good friends for a long time. Always had fun together, and I thought that was all it was. Now I'm not so sure." He kissed me again. "No," he whispered, "not sure at all. We'd have fun, child. Think about it. You might enjoy being married to me, and I believe I would be happy to pass the rest of my years in your prickly, lively and charming company."

He removed his arm and pulled out his wallet and wrote on one of his cards. "Keep this, sweet. I don't know what I could do from two counties away, but send for me if you need me, and I'll come faster than the west wind itself."

I was astonished and touched and managed to squeeze his hand while he helped me pull out the bundle. "I'll let you know," I promised. "And I'll think about it, truly. And thanks for everything."

He made a V sign and drove away. I strolled along the gardens, around the courtyard to the door by the back stairs. More than once I had hidden forbidden objects in the black angle behind the steep steps, and I could think of no better place now. Then I went along to my room, blessing again Cousin Aylmer and his desire not to hear, or have others hear, any sound of footsteps in the halls. Dear Charles, I thought as I changed, how nice of him. What a surprise, but how good for my ego. I felt quite set up. He meant it now, I could feel, but for how long? If I needed him . . . well, the thought was comforting. As for my immediate problem, I had motive and means for my activities, all I needed was opportunity, and that had better come that very night.

My first care was the pictures themselves. When everyone was safely involved in tea, I sped to the attic and the trunk. As I wrapped and tied the paintings in the plastic I hoped I was being gentle enough so that there would be no real damage. They made a bulky package but not a heavy one and could easily be carried in that shopping bag. I locked the trunk, stuck the bag in the

end of the wardrobe in my room, where the black kept it
from being obvious to anyone who opened the door, and
arrived for tea apologizing for oversleeping. No one paid
me any attention, and I wondered if that was a good sign
or a bad one, or if they were just annoyed at me for having kept so much secret for so long. But what I had been
doing in London was really none of their business, and
they never would have asked or cared except for Charles.
My heart warmed to him.

Amaury crossed to sit beside me. "When you think of
something that pleases you a sort of glow comes over
you, Petra. What is it this time?"

I denied the glow and said something about roses and
turned him aside. Roger came for dinner again and we
played bridge. He looked very stoic and solemn all evening, for though Isabelle said and did nothing untoward,
it was obvious she was following Nico wherever he
moved, listening to everything he said, and playing
poorly whether she was at his table, or another. He
seemed oblivious of it all and was not only exuding
charm but also a little above himself, just a touch excited, I thought, about something ahead, and I wondered
uneasily what. Once I caught Cousin Eugenia watching
Isabelle as she watched Nico. Eugenia, intent, concentrated, as though trying to convey a message, and without any mask over her face, looked haggard and un-
lovely. For the first time I glimpsed what Alexandra had
meant. Of course it was a fearful blow to have her one
lamb, her swan, her own hope for her future unwed
after four years out and now falling for a foreigner
without a fortune, even if he was a Montluc and a
relative in a way. But it was her own fault, I told myself,

and she deserved the disappointment ahead, though I was not sure now Isabelle did.

When we stopped playing and were having nightcaps, Gavin edged me toward the front windows. "You give me an uneasy feeling," he began, with a lilt in his voice and an amused gleam in those surprising gray eyes. "I've been wondering what you are storing up here for your next story or play."

I laughed delightedly. "Neither I, nor anyone else, could give you an uneasy feeling, and you know it."

He looked startled but laughed in turn. "Oh, much does. You can't imagine. But I did want to say I've read several of your tales and enjoyed them. I never had any thought they were by, well, a lady author."

"That's one of the nicest things you could say," I told him, feeling that glow Amaury had claimed I was showing. "I didn't want anyone to think they were, of course. I'm glad you liked them." He could be so nice at times, I wished he would be always.

"You're really serious about writing, aren't you?" he asked with a tinge of wonder.

"Of course. That's how I support myself, and the best way I've found. I had so many different kinds of work those first years that when I began writing short stories I naturally used what I knew: shops, big and small, business offices, an art gallery, a girls' school. Then I graduated to light mysteries and comedies. I've been thankful in some ways it wasn't all made easy."

"Yes. I've heard something of you from Alexandra, recently. All you've missed is being a lady bobby or a double spy!"

"Don't be too sure about that," I said gaily, though

falsely. "It's always well to keep people guessing." He looked so startled that I laughed again. "Don't worry about my using Aylforth. I love it too much to make capital out of it."

"But the people?" he probed.

"That's different. Who knows?" I evaded. "Doesn't that depend on the future?" And I left him.

The nursery was the southeast corner of the second floor. The three mullioned windows above the window seat looked out to the front of the house, down the terrace and drive to the oak wood. On the east side another window, considerably larger, had been cut at some later date. This was the one I had always used for escape.

The hours dragged as I waited. A night can be open and shut as much as a day, and this one had the moon coming out, nearly full, at times, and then vanishing behind masses of soft clouds that filtered but did not hide the light. It was one o'clock before I dared move. There was no sound in the house when I opened my door to reconnoiter before using the skeleton key to lock it from the inside, and no light came from the rooms on the front. Of course I could not see Gavin's study or his room above it, but then he could not see me. I tried to summon the Saint to my side as I got ready and realized with a hollow feeling he wouldn't come. He had left me for good, and henceforth I would be on my own. I hadn't time to ask myself why.

But the old familiar precautions came back. I rolled up my blanket and pillow in the bed and tied the thicker rope tightly to the leg nearest the window. The bed had been heavy enough to hold me before, I hoped it would now. I put the torch in the carryall with the paintings and lowered it by the light rope, pulled on my dark slacks and sweater, tied a scarf over my head, and put on my crepe-soled shoes, and with the rope in my right hand edged out of the window and felt for the first of the stepping stones at the corner, put there by the builders for their convenience in going up and down the outside of the house. Though ivy had grown over some, they were there and solid. I was quickly down and looped the ropes into the ivy so they would not show. Then, carryall on my left arm, I set out around the house and gardens, keeping off the gravel, for the back path to the ruins of Marden Castle.

The moon helped me find where the path left the lane, which was as well, for I planned not to use my torch in the open. Anyone, even Constable Tompkins, might see it and decide to investigate. In some spots the path was bushier than before, in some more clear where bushes had grown into small trees, and then it was open through the roughness of unused fields. My feet knew the way as well as my mind, and if night noises could not bother me ten years ago, they could not now. Or so I told myself as something squeaked nearby and was silent when an owl hooted. A fox barked and a bird squawked once. The gray light worked very well for me, particularly in the open, and except for the fact that I was moving I did not think anyone who might be night-walking would notice my dark figure.

The ruins seemed swathed in shadows as I climbed over the turnstile. The paved path carried me so quickly to the entrance that I did not have time to begin to panic. But, I told myself, I wouldn't have anyway. The keep inside was, at first, completely black, but as I waited I could see the fainter blackness of the windows and sky overhead. But the crypt, cellar, whatever they wished to call it, now, that would be truly blackness personified. Very slowly I swiveled and looked where I knew the doorway waited. No one could be expected to walk through that impenetrable wall, I decided flatly. I leaned against the stones beside me and breathed deeply as I once did before going on stage. If I didn't go there, I'd have to carry the things back, and back into danger for them and me. I found the torch and shielding the bulb with one hand, switched it on. Even muffled, the light was so bright I actually hastened forward lest it show beyond the walls and entrance, and hurried down those nice new solid stairs. Once below, I let more light seep through my fingers, though the door above was at an angle to the outer wall and the light could not really be seen, except by chance.

The fireplace was so low that I had to kneel to peer up into the chimney, which was narrow and wide but not deep. The torch showed it quite black with soot, but also revealed a little ledge where the stone of the mantel jutted through a few inches. It was enough to hold the carryall. And if it should rain, the carryall and then the plastic should protect the paintings from any drops the chimney itself did not deflect. I stowed the bag in place. Anyone would have to get inside to find it. My hands were quite black by the time I finished. I'd have to wipe them on the dew of the grass, in some inconspicuous spot, and shake my clothes. I poked the carryall; it sat there firmly. Some soot pattered as I backed away.

Amaury had dislodged so much with his probing, a little more would not matter. There were so many footprints in the dust, mine would not show; in fact, nothing showed. Satisfied, I hurried up the stairs and put out the torch.

So lighthearted was I on the return trip I started to whistle, but stopped quickly. That could call attention as much as a light on such a still night. At the edge of the wood was long grass, so I moved from the path and wiped off as much soot as I could and shook the scarf and sweater and hoped most of it was gone. It was easier to go up the rope and the stones than to come down, and again I blessed those Tudor masons who had had the sense to build the stones in firmly for their own convenience. The ropes came up easily and were stowed in a paper bag on the top of the wardrobe behind the ornamental front where, obviously, no one had dusted in years. Some soot clung to the wet shoes; I'd have to dust them carefully when they were dry, but there was only a little left on my hands. In the morning I'd go over my clothes.

Feeling more safe and at ease than at any time since I had come, I unlocked my door, and dropped into bed. I had been gone not much over an hour.

11

As I bathed and dressed I began to think about what I should do next. I almost wished I could leave Aylforth and stay away until after the Montlucs departed and I could turn the paintings over to a re-covered Mr. Thetwin. Nico and his cohorts were danger-ous and determined men and brought danger with them, I was sure. But I had a trust and a duty; I couldn't leave. As a precaution, I could write an account to Charles, but then would come the problem of mailing it without a watcher at my elbow to stop me. I could find out about that, for there was Mrs. Carrick, who had not yet received her picture and pin. A visit to her would be some kind of a test.

As the others were lingering over coffee at breakfast when I came down, I announced it was high time I carried out my last errand.

"Splendid," agreed Nico. "We'll all go with you. See something of the countryside. You'd like to go, wouldn't you, Isabelle?"

She nodded, her eyes showing she'd go anywhere he asked.

"And before we go," he went on gaily, "would you mind terribly if we looked in that trunk of Nanny's? Amaury and I were checking over things last night and realized that was the one place we had not searched. Of course it's probably quite unnecessary, but just to finish the job. . . . May we?"

"Of course," I agreed amiably. "I'll get the key in a minute. There are two chests in the attic, too, but I didn't see anything but dolls in them."

After breakfast I handed Nico the key. I had pushed the lining in the valise down to the bottom, so now it merely looked nearly empty, or so I hoped. As they left, Isabelle drifted over. "You're sure you don't mind our going with you?"

It was so unusual, or had been, for her to wonder about the feelings of anyone else that I was touched. "Of course not," I assured her warmly, "though you'll all be bored by the reminiscences. You'd better keep the men entertained in the car while I visit with Mrs. Carrick." She looked touchingly grateful at the suggestion.

So I went for the box with the pin and the picture and met the Montlucs in the hall. "You're right." Nico handed me the trunk key. "Nothing in the chests or trunk. We did wonder, though," and he watched me with hard eyes, "if anything had been hidden under the lining of that old valise. Did Nanny ever say anything to you about that?"

"No." I shook my head. I always prefer to be truthful. "What do you mean?"

"Oh, we started to pull it up—obvious place, you know —and it came out quite easily." He saw nothing in his conduct, but his assumption that he could do such a thing and talk about it calmly and no one would object was infuriating.

"There's a dress and suit that must have belonged to Mother," Amaury broke in. "They . . . they look like her."

Nico was watching him under lowered lids. My sense of outrage at him did not extend to Amaury.

"I'm sure they belonged to her," I said gently. "She must have left them with Nanny, hoping to use them later."

"I had the same thought," murmured Nico. "Could almost see her in them."

"Oh, no." Amaury looked at him in surprise. "I'm quite certain these were the new clothes she brought back from Paris that last time. She never had a chance to wear them. But Father had helped her choose them. She must have wanted to keep them because of that."

Nico shrugged. "Whatever you say. You spent more time with her; you remember better."

"Quite," said Amaury tightly and turned to me with what was meant for a grin. "Lucky you don't play with dolls any more, Petra. We thought something might be hidden in one of them, a letter, perhaps, so they're a bit damaged now." He was challenging me to object. "I started, but Nico helped. There was nothing, of course."

Intent on my own experiment, I didn't really take in what he was saying. "Let's go. It shouldn't take us long."

It took longer than it might have, for I kept to main roads and doubled the journey. The black sedan followed, then passed us quickly and disappeared. There was my answer. Mrs. Carrick was touched by the presents and tearful at my visit. A neat daughter-in-law, brusque yet loving, patted her on the back and told her to pull herself together, then went back to her baking so we could talk for half an hour. The three outside were not at all impatient, and we returned sedately. At least I knew I wouldn't be going anywhere alone for a while. But that by itself proved nothing. I could only wait.

After lunch I decided on a nap; I was beginning to miss that lost sleep. Amaury strolled into the hall and watched me to my room. When all was quiet below, I went to the attic, for Amaury's word returned to me. I had left several of the dolls sitting on top of one chest, Melissa and Catherine and a rag doll I had called Polly Waggletail until Nanny made me change her name to Jane. Now they lay in a row, each cut open by one stroke of a knife, their rags and stuffing spilling around about them. All those inside the chest had been treated the same way and one large porcelain doll of Isabelle's, Vanessa as I remembered, had even been decapitated to be sure her hollow head was as empty as her beaming face. I tiptoed to the far dark corner and lifted one side of the blackout curtain. Elizabeth and Winnie lay undisturbed. That was good in its own way, but my hands shook as I put all the other dolls back in the chest. I did not like this at all. The two must have vented their rage this way and found excitement and satisfaction as they did. This was something to tell Gavin. Such violence seemed quite terrifying. The thought of Gavin comforted me as I fell asleep. I'd see him soon.

I was so confident that I was not surprised when we met at the top of the stairs on our way to tea. The others could be heard below. I put my finger on my lips and motioned him into the nursery and shut the door. Showing him something wasn't asking for help.

"What's the matter, Petra?" His voice was gentle.

"Go look at the dolls in the chest in the attic," I stammered, as much unnerved by his concern as by the memory. He nodded, left, and was back in a moment. Once more the aquiline face was without expression. "Tell me," he ordered.

I did, steadied by his presence. He gathered up my two hands and held them in his. "It's unpleasant. An impulse of frustration, I'm sure." His voice was calm but I knew he liked it as little as I did, and realized it had been deliberate destruction. His hands tightened as I shook my head. "All right. I shan't pretend. It is more than unpleasant. But we can't do anything but watch and wait for the explosion, which must come soon. Now"—he bent and his lips brushed my cheek—"go down and have tea and say nothing. I'll be along." It was comforting to know he shared my feeling. Security flooded around me and I obeyed.

The three others were looking gay and excited and Isabelle smug to boot. "I remembered, Petra," she called gaily as I crossed the room. "You know I never remember *anything*, but this time I did, something you forgot."

"What?" I asked, but there was only one place left unexplored.

"The secret room. The one back of the chimney in the banquet hall! You'll remember now. Cousin Aylmer showed it to us one rainy afternoon. And I could find how to open it, too."

"But not how to get out," added Nico laughing. "I had to put my shoe in the door."

Isabelle smiled proudly as if no one had ever had such a bright idea before, and repeated the whole tale to Gavin, who was suitably impressed.

"I remember, too, now," Cousin Alexandra remarked. "But I'm sure I no longer know the places to press to open the door. We used to play cavaliers and roundheads there, even when we were quite grown. I always thought of ghosts . . . it was quite delicious."

Then they had to tell us all about it, and the fruitless search which took a good deal of time but seemed to please them. I thought of saying something, anything, to Cousin Alexandra to warn her of I knew not what, but Sloane drove up with her letters and she swept out to the terrace to meet him.

As we were crossing the hall to dinner, the front-door gong rang, something so unusual that we all stopped. Manson opened it on two figures. "Constable Tompkins and a person to see you, sir," he told Gavin, with disapproval.

So lean and distinguished in his black and white dinner clothes that my heart gave a surprising lurch, Gavin moved from beside Cousin Eugenia as Constable Tompkins entered, his hand on the shoulder of a nondescript man in a dark-brown suit.

"Sorry to trouble you, sir"—the constable removed his cap quickly—"but this person was lurking at the gate as I came by. Ran into the bushes when I stopped and I 'ad to pull him out. Said he had a package for one of the gentlemen 'ere." He paused. He was a stocky man and filled his uniform well, but not with fat. His face was long and solemn, his hair going gray, his eyes guileless, but I knew he could practically see out of the back of his head when a small boy behind him was stealing an apple from a stand, and that he had us all docketed and filed away.

"Quite right, Constable," Gavin assured him cordially. "What do you have, and who's it for?"

The constable swung around with a muttered "Mind your manners now," and jerked the cap from the head of the man behind him. He looked local and not very bright as he glanced around our group and back to Gavin. "A package, sir, for Mr. Nicholas Montluc. Man from London give me five bob to bring it up here 'cause 'e didn't 'ave time to stop and look for the place 'imself." He held out a small white package. "And no call for you to jerk a man up for making a bit of change, neither," he added to Mr. Tompkins irately.

"Is it possible?" Gavin asked of the constable. "Have you seen this man before?"

Constable Tompkins teetered a little back and forth and nodded. "Yes, to both, sir. There's plenty of cars going through these days; some stop for a bite; some don't. So it could be. And I've seen 'im about on occasion. Comes from Verwood way, I think; odd jobs he might be doing, but I know nothing about 'im, really."

Nico moved forward, all suave grace. "May I see if the box is really for me?" He took it, examined it and slipped it in the pocket of his jacket. "Yes. Something I ordered. But I hardly expected it to be delivered this way. Here," he pulled a coin from his pocket and dropped it in the man's hand, "for your trouble." His hand moved to his pocket again as he looked at Mr. Tompkins, who shook his head. "Oh, no, sir, nothing like that, you should know."

. . . . *167*

"Thank you very much, Constable," Gavin interposed quickly. "You were quite right to bring the man to the house. Perhaps you'll be good enough to see him out the gate and then come back for a beer with Mrs. Mellowfield."

"Thank *you*, sir." Tompkins shoved his cap back on his head. "I'll just see 'im to the village. I'll take you up on the beer some other time, if I may, sir. Still 'ave my rounds to make."

"Any time, of course," approved Gavin.

The two left and we hastened to dinner. The soup was still warm; it had all passed so quickly.

"Sorry to have caused such a commotion," Nico said airily as he laid down his spoon. He looked apologetically at Gavin, then winked at Amaury. There was something about him that made me uneasy, and I was glad my expedition last night had been so successful.

Nico began to talk. Gradually and carefully he became the life of the party, first by telling some genuinely amusing tales of his experiences in Paris and at St. Tropez, where he had met Brigitte Bardot and other Riviera denizens and viewed them all as a wide-eyed stranger who had been away from France for a long time. He recounted his stories with verve and wit—I could only admire his performance—and we were still laughing when we left the dining room. The coffee was hardly cleared before he had us all playing games, first a paper-and-word game and then a kind of charade I was sure he invented, for it was adapted so well for us all. Even Gavin entered wholeheartedly and did an impersonation of a French Canadian trapper in a country store that was very funny. I was so happy to see he could be light and gay that I forgot my apprehensions. It was quite eleven before Cousin Alexandra called a halt, saying she was exhausted but had not enjoyed an evening so much in years. Eugenia was flushed and bright-eyed, and it was apparent that she might even have been pretty in her youth—the thought was a new one to me. Someone murmured "Bridge," and the two ladies left us, with Gavin following slowly, still watching us as he went out the door.

Nico gestured us into the morning room. I thought this was because it was more cozy and quiet, but when he closed the door carefully behind us, my apprehensions returned. His eyes were too bright, his color too high, yet he was suddenly cool and in command. He and Amaury drew chairs into a circle and practically pushed me down in the corner of the sofa. Isabelle just watched him happily. Amaury was intent on us both. I wished for Gavin.

Turning a straight chair around, Nico sat down with his arms across the back, facing us. "No need to go into why we're here or our lack of success in finding what we came for," he began, like a chairman at a board meeting. "We all know, too, that it's evident now that Petra is the key to our search, but she could not, or would not, remember what was needed. We thought"—he glanced at Amaury, who nodded—"that with time she might be willing to help us, or reveal by accident what she knows. But she hasn't. Yet she's been leaving her room at night, though we only caught up with her once. We've decided we can wait no longer. So I thought of a way to help her. I could have done it differently, but Amaury wouldn't let me." His smile mocked us both.

He wouldn't be diverted, I knew, but if I could gain a little time, anything might happen. There was something I wanted to know; it had been in my mind since my encounter with Gavin. "What *did* the note the Princess left here say?" I asked.

"Not enough to help us," Amaury answered. "Mother wrote that she needed advice about some things she had left here and would come down again when she could, or Maxim or someone she trusted would come in her place." That was definite, anyway, and helped explain their persistence.

"We're wasting time," Nico broke in. "No more asking Petra. She's going to tell us here and now what she knows."

This I did not like at all. I am more susceptible than would be expected to medicine, drugs, even hypnosis. "No crystal balls," I said quickly.

He waved his hand in scorn. "Nothing so silly as that. I remembered the truth drug, scopolamine. Police use it, doctors too. Doesn't do any harm, but it does make a person talk about things he doesn't know he knows. I sent for some, and a hypodermic, and that was the parcel that came this evening. We're going to give a dose to Petra."

"No." I sat up. "You've no right. I'll not let you."

"You haven't any choice. You can't stop us."

"But I wouldn't say anything about the Princess—there's nothing. What would come would be all sorts of odds and ends."

"I doubt it. We've all talked and thought so much about those bloody paintings, wherever they are, that they're bound to be on top of your subconscious. It's our only chance." He rose. "Isabelle and I will go to the kitchen to sterilize the needle. Everything will be done according to the safest modern methods, you see. Then, if Petra hasn't remembered anything by the time we get back, I'll just give her the hypo in that pretty right arm of hers and we'll wait for her to talk! It doesn't take more than five minutes for the stuff to work. Once she gives the clue, we're off."

He put out a hand to Isabelle, who rose obediently, and pulled out a white box. Inside, as he showed me, there was indeed a hypodermic syringe and needle, an ampul, cotton, and a tiny vial of alcohol. It was all very neat and shipshape.

"No!" I cried again. "I'll scream."

"No one'll hear you, particularly if Amaury puts a pillow over your face. Don't be a stupid fool. We're going to do it; it'll do you no harm; you'll be better off if you cooperate with us instead of fighting us." His voice was so cold that for the first time Isabelle looked at him questioningly. "Of course it may all come to you in a blinding flash meanwhile," he added sarcastically. "Keep her here and *quiet*, Amaury," he ordered. Isabelle trailed him out of the room and shut the door.

I was truly frightened. I knew enough to realize the drug wouldn't hurt me, but also that I'd probably give everything away. The whole idea revolted me. I must think. . . . I was in the corner of the couch with my back to the windows. A small baroque mirror next to the door faced me. I must think of something. . . .

Amaury came over and sat down beside me and put a hand on my knee. "Don't try to get away, Petra," he warned. "Old Nico's on his high horse and absolutely determined. And I have a feeling he can be a pretty unpleasant customer these days. Wouldn't it be better to talk . . . no drug or piqûre or anything like that?''

Should I tell him? I wondered wildly. Would that do any good? Suppose I told him his brother wasn't Nico? But clever Nico would get around that. My stubborn streak kept me quiet. I had vowed to myself I would protect the pictures of the Princess from Nico and his men. I couldn't just give in weakly now. I stirred as if to get up, and the large hand tightened as it covered mine. "Don't try it. I wouldn't even have to use a pillow to keep you quiet. I could do it this way."

He loomed over me and kissed me, long and hard. When he lifted his head, his eyes were gleaming. "You're most attractive, Petra. Especially when you're frightened. Each day I've liked you more. Nico used to say I was a madman sometimes—come, be mad with me.''

I shook my head and moved, and both hands came down heavily on my thigh. "Keep quiet," he growled.

I *had* to get away. I straightened and swung my right leg over my left. A kick on the shin might disconcert him just enough. A hand on my breast pushed me back into the corner, and the tanned face with its queer, intent look came closer. I gasped, and was almost glad to have the door open. By the time they entered Amaury had straightened up and swung me around so I was sitting with an arm on the back of the sofa.

They had brought everything, including a small saucepan in which they had sterilized the needle. Nico's bright smile was no longer attractive. "Don't worry, Cousin. I've done this often before, so I won't make a slip and hurt you. But don't move, or I might."

Isabelle looked troubled but was still obedient. They put everything on the narrow table top, which was level with the back of the sofa. Amaury left his chair and moved behind me. I watched in horrid fascination as Nico fitted in the needle, broke the ampul and filled the hypo and propped it slanting against a book, then opened the vial to a faint scent of alcohol. Eyes intent, he moistened a piece of cotton. And I thought of one of the oldest dodges, one I'd used long ago in a story. My left arm was hanging beside the sofa. I gave a thump on the frame, looked beyond the table, and lifted my right hand and pointed to the door.

"Someone's coming," I croaked.

Three heads turned to the door. Amaury tiptoed toward it. I dropped my right hand, seized the hypodermic, turned it to the side, and pushed the plunger so the liquid ran down between the back of the sofa and the table until only a fourth of the drug remained, then let it fall back into place. There was only one ampul. I must trust the reduced dose would have little or no effect and that the loss of the liquid would not be noticed.

It wasn't. When no one entered the room and Amaury, peering into the hall, announced all clear, Nico was so furious at me that he just dabbed at my skin, seized the hypo, and thrust the needle in so hard it hurt. I cried out, which both pleased and distracted him. His glance moved to my face, and I felt he would like to do much more to me than stick me with a short needle.

"Now we'll just wait." He pushed me back in my corner and put the things back in the box.

I closed my eyes. Five minutes, he had said it took to work. What could I say that would satisfy them and yet

lead them astray? Nothing came to mind. I must think
—and I couldn't. I was drowsy, I realized. Even such a
small amount could have some effect on me. The room
was still except for our breathing. The whole house was
still except for faint breathing sounds everywhere. But
the dolls wouldn't be breathing.

To my surprise I heard myself say, "Dolls," and from
a floating distance an eerie satisfied voice said, "That
bothered her. I thought it would."

I shifted my head. I mustn't think. Light and dark
were turning in circles under my lids. I must have gone
out for a moment. I came to, horrified, to hear myself
saying, "Black . . . fireplace . . . hide . . ." I hadn't
been able to help it, I told myself muzzily. Nothing more
came out. The shock seemed to begin to bring me back
a bit.

"Aaaahh." That was Nico. "Something's hidden in a
fireplace. It's got to be the paintings. Where?" Dimly I
heard Isabelle give a sob.

"What are you doing to Petra?" The anger in the voice
penetrated, and I raised heavy eyelids. Gavin seemed so
tall he reached the ceiling. I wondered dreamily how he
had come in the door.

"Just an experiment, Gavin," Nico said smoothly, "to
help her remember—what she knows. She's been helpful."

"This is outrageous. You have no right to use drugs on
her. That's what this syringe is for, isn't it? I'm calling
the police."

"Stand still."

He was giving Gavin an order! I made my eyes move,
and they came to rest on a revolver in Nico's hand
pointed at me! The room fell quiet. "We know quite well

what we're doing. You better not interfere. If you try to, I'll shoot her, perhaps not fatally but unpleasantly."

I closed my eyes again. I could hear better that way. Isabelle was crying steadily now.

Nico the organizer went on giving orders. "Amaury, open that window for Louis. He's been enjoying the so-charming terrace, after bringing the car for us." A breeze swept through the room, followed by steps. "Good. We probably won't need either your brains or your gun, but have both ready. Amaury, take this key and lock those two old biddies in their rooms upstairs, also the cook and the maid. We can't have any of them interfering, now things are moving. *Dear* Amaury," he chuckled. "Go along. We can wait. The laird here won't move with two guns on Petra."

How silly, I thought, as if that would stop him—and let the colors shift before my eyes, but more slowly. Dimly I heard Nico say to Isabelle, "Sorry, sweet, but this is important, you know. I'll explain later. But I can't let your kind heart interfere."

I lost Isabelle's murmur. Someone had said, "Pull yourself together." That's what I must do.

Amaury was back. A key clicked on the table. "Every door locked, including the servants'. Glad all the men sleep out. Manson's finishing his chores."

"Now," Nico began, didactically, "there are a lot of fireplaces in the house but only two which have not been used for years: the one in the banqueting hall and the one in the secret room. Petra didn't remember about the secret room—she looked surprised when we spoke of it. We searched that, but not the chimney, but it's small. The one in the hall seems the most likely. We'll take that first. But we'll use the little room to keep these two quiet and out of our way.''

The colors were gone, but I felt sleepy. My eyes closed.

"Look here, Nico," I heard Gavin, the reasonable, civilized man, begin quietly. "What's all this about? Why threaten Petra?"

"We're not threatening her, just using her at the moment to keep you quiet. She's told us, thanks to a wonder drug called scopolamine—ever hear of it?—that there's something hidden in a black fireplace. We're going to find it; that's all."

"All right. The pictures are yours, if that's what's hidden. No one objects to your finding them. But all this rush isn't necessary."

"But it is, now we know. We have . . . well . . . appointments. We've wasted too much time because we tried to do it all in a *nice* way, though it's results that count. But these paintings are worth all the trouble."

"Watteau," I murmured, without meaning to.

"See?" he exulted. "She did know about them, hide them. Kept them secret. The little bitch."

Oh, dear, I told myself. I shouldn't have said that. I made my eyelids rise far enough to look at Gavin. His face showed nothing, his eyes were downcast, but one pulse pounded in his cheek. "All right," he said. "Go get them and get out. But leave Petra, us, alone." I let my lids fall.

"And have you calling the police in two minutes?"

"I give you my word I won't."

"Do not trust him," grated the voice of the man in the black car.

"I don't trust any of them. It'll be quite a while before

these three are found in that convenient secret room. We'll have plenty of time for everything.''

"Petra's staying right here on the couch," Amaury said flatly. "She's out completely, probably for hours."

"Have it your way," Nico agreed with surprising quickness. "Gavin, Louis and I are taking you and Isabelle to the secret room and putting you in. Don't try anything; we both have guns, and we've never minded using them. Amaury can stay here with Petra, since he's so fond of her. We'll know where to get him if we need him."

I heard the four leave. I heard steps and Manson saying, "Where are they?" and Amaury answering, "In the banqueting hall. Nico'll want your help there."

Then it was truly quiet. Now I could sleep.

My face was being slapped with a wet towel and brandy was being held to my mouth. "Come on, Petra," Amaury was urging. "Wake up. You aren't really out. Oh, you clever girl. I saw you in the mirror. You emptied that syringe. Nico never noticed. Joke's on him. Here. Sit up."

He patted my face and poured more brandy down me. "But you couldn't help giving away one thing, could you? That stuff does work. I was against it until Nico swore it wouldn't hurt you. And now that so-smart brother thinks he knows. He's wrong, isn't he? Lovely Petra! He and Louis and Manson are working away at that huge fireplace, trying to take it apart. Wish I could go and laugh at them.

"But you and I have something else to do. We're going right now to Marden Castle. You're going to drive because you know the way in the dark. I'll know if you're going the right way. I want you with me, and I couldn't drive and hold a gun on you too, could I? And when we're at the tower, you're going to show me which of those three fireplaces you used, so we won't waste any time. We'll be off before Nico knows he's been foxed. Oh, I'll see he gets his share, but it's those other two I want to cut out."

The cold water and the brandy did bring me around. I shook my head. But Amaury picked me up and ran with me down the corridor to the courtyard, where my Austin was parked. He made me walk the last bit, and I could, to my surprise, and I could also focus. There was enough light from the coming moon to help. I couldn't get away from him. If I refused to drive, he'd just knock me out and dump me in the back seat and drive himself, I felt sure.

"Might be a mistake to bring you," he told me as he shoved me behind the wheel, " but it will save time. And it'll put the wind up old Nico for sure . . . and those others."

12

He helped me start the car and get into the lane and held his right hand ready to seize the wheel if I made a false turn. Once he put down the revolver while he fumbled in the glove compartment and brought out the torch I always leave there. "Found this when I searched your car. I told myself then my cousin was a very prudent girl, but I see you're much more than that." He chuckled, then prodded me. "Laugh, Cousin, that was funny. But don't forget to put off your lights when you turn down that track to the castle."

I snorted obediently at the joke and in a few minutes put out the lights and ran carefully down the lane to the little car park below the ruin.

"Turn the car around so it faces away, but put it under the shadow of that oak," he directed, "and leave the keys above the visor in case we need to make a quick getaway, though there isn't much chance of that." He chuckled again. "Old Nico is so thorough when his mind is set on something, it will take him quite a while to find he's been diddled. He'll keep those two hard at work."

He put the torch in his pocket, took my arm, and we climbed over the turnstile and up the slope. My head was clearer, but my legs were still wobbly. Once inside the keep he stopped, holding my arm and the torch with one hand. A light wind swept through the entrance, caught up a little dust in a swirl and fled up and out the open trapdoor at the top of the tower.

"Which one of these did you use?" Amaury asked tensely. Dragging me first to one, then the other, he shook his head. "No fallen soot. There would be if you'd hidden anything inside a chimney. Now, down we go." He hustled me to the guardroom below. The fallen soot below the chimney became a heavy scattering of black in the light of the torch. "It looks natural, though," he approved. "No one would guess but me. Now just go over there and bring out the package or whatever it is."

"Why don't you go get it?" I whispered. "I can't walk alone."

He shook his head reprovingly. "You think I'd fall for that? Oh, no. Once I got my head inside that chimney, you'd run away. Go along. I don't want to hurt you, but—" Suddenly my arm was twisted up behind my back, so I gave a yelp. "Be a good girl, and we'll be off in a minute."

The shadows leaned forward to watch as I walked unsteadily down the beam of the torch. I stepped inside the fireplace, twisted, and brought down the black carry-all and some more soot. He seized it from me as I tried to shake the soot from my hair and looked surprised at the weight. "So many?"

"Five," I said dully.

He laughed exuberantly. "Good show. I must take a

look. We'll take the time. They must be fabulous—trust my sagacious mother.''

He slung the bag on his arm, seized mine again, and rushed me up the stairs into the keep. After a quick glance at the entrance he pulled me to the angle under the new cement stairs and pressed me down so that I sat in the dust. He hunkered beside me, the torch in his left hand, pistol in his right. ''Open up. I must see,'' he ordered.

One by one I unwrapped the pictures, to a running murmur of delight. ''Yes, I remember the Watteaus. Mother brought them from Hungary and kept them in her room. Yes, the Van Gogh was in the nursery because it was so cheerful. Father liked the Chardin and the Monet. I wonder what the others were. You're sure there were no more?'' He brooded as I wrapped them back in their pillowcases and plastic. ''There were, once, you could tell from the space left in that valise. But we're lucky to have these. Uncle will be so pleased—and I can have my farm.''

''What are you going to do about Nico?'' I asked. Something was still wrong with my head, for I thought I heard faraway hoofbeats.

He gave a hoot. ''Dear brother can look out for himself. He always has. But we'll see he gets a share, but not those two.'' He laughed loudly. ''It's almost too good to be true—I have the pictures and I have you.'' One arm gathered me to him. His face nuzzled my neck. ''I liked you the minute I saw you in the hall. Always have preferred pretty, plucky girls. But you're more than that, and I'm crazy about you now. One kiss and we'll be off for France.''

. . . . 181

He loosened his hold to kiss me and I pushed myself back out of his arms and up on my feet. He sprang up, dropping pistol and torch to the dust, and reached for me. I'd been pushed around enough. I drew back and slapped his face hard. "No. I wouldn't have anything to do with you if you owned the Louvre," I cried.

His surprise was so comical I laughed. At that the pale eyes narrowed, and he drew in his breath in a whistle. "Don't get above yourself. I won't be mocked."

The icy glitter of his eyes frightened me. Norman, Saxon, Dane, Tartar, who knew what blood had gone into the makeup of this man? He was no longer the pleasant Amaury. As his hand, three times its size in the light and shadow, reached for me, I jumped and ran.

Quick as a cat, he was before me at the entrance. That left only the stairs. If I could get to the platform at the top I could drop and bolt the trapdoor. He wouldn't push that up in a hurry, strong as he was; I could wait on the platform for daylight and rescue. I swung around and was up the stairs to the small platform on the first-floor level before he realized what I intended. My knees began to shake and I halted.

Swinging the torch, he stepped lightly to the spot below me, looked up and laughed. "You're still above yourself," he chided, but his eyes hadn't lost their glitter. "You know I'll have you, sooner or later. If you don't come down, I'll come up and get you."

I shook my head and backed toward the next flight of steps. He set the torch firmly upright in the soft dirt below and began to mount.

He was a third of the way up and I was stumbling at the first step of the next flight when a man hurtled through the entrance. It was Gavin. I sagged against the wall. Amaury was below on the stairs. Gavin couldn't follow him up, for he'd be at too great a disadvantage.

"Stay still," Gavin called. "I'm coming."

Amaury laughed. "Go home, Gavin. You've lost. Give up."

I wanted to shout about the revolver in the dust, but it was nearer Amaury. The granite wall was rough and cold beneath my hands.

Casually, Gavin turned his back and began to mount the broken remnants of the old stairs that still rose on the opposite wall and turned halfway toward the platform where I stood. Amaury was still watching me and laughing and did not see the moment when Gavin flung himself across from the crumbling stones to the railing of the platform, caught it, swung himself over, brushed by me and launched himself down on the man beneath him. They rolled over and over to the floor and lay still. My back to the wall, I edged after them.

Then both were on their feet. Amaury leaped at Gavin, who backed into the center, brought up one arm and sidestepped. His fist landed on Amaury's cheek, but Amaury whirled, fists raised. I must get the gun, though if I did I couldn't use it; any shot might hit the wrong man. They were pummeling, dodging, circling, while shadows rose and fell on the walls. Amaury's eyes blazed; he was fighting for the sheer joy of it—and for his booty. When he knocked Gavin down and shouted in triumph, I found I had expected it. This was the Norseman gone berserk. But Gavin was up again, blood running from his forehead. Still the reasonable man, his face grim, gray eyes intent, he was the dark Scot doing a job that had to be done. But I was afraid for him, more than I had been for myself. If I could rush in and catch one of Amaury's legs and throw him . . . If only he didn't remember the revolver. Watching them, I stole toward it, picked it up and began to creep forward to where they were now stolidly slugging each other.

"Gentlemen, gentlemen. What's going on 'ere?"

This time it was Constable Tompkins who came striding into the keep. I noticed another dim figure behind him. The two men did not hear. Tompkins moved quickly and, a hand on each shoulder, by plain strength jerked them apart. Both were bleeding.

"Let me alone, you fool," Amaury panted.

"Now, now," Tompkins chided. "Disturbing the peace. We'll just go along down to the gaol and book you."

"It won't be necessary, Constable." Gavin was gasping but his first glance had been for me. "We were just settling a difference."

"No way to do it, Mr. Langlade." The austere tone was reproving.

"But private, you know." Gavin was still jerking out his words. "We were on a treasure hunt—and disagreed."

In the light of the torch Tompkins' face folded into heavy lines. "As you say, sir. But we'll have to charge you."

"There's no charge." Gavin became authoritative, between gasps, and the constable dropped his hand. "There's a lady here. Can't we all go back to the Priory and talk it over?"

Tompkins looked over at me, stepped to my side, and

took the revolver from my hand. "Now, miss, that's not the proper thing for a young lady to carry."

The tone called back all the years when I had been doing things not proper for a young lady. Perhaps he remembered, too, for he softened. "Very well, Mr. Langlade. How did you get here, miss?"

"Car," I said faintly.

"Very good. You rode, sir? I'll release you on your word to return at once to the Priory."

Gavin nodded and pulled out a handkerchief and began to tap at his face where it was bleeding. I wanted to help him, and to thank him for coming. He looked at me anxiously. "Are you all right, Petra? That warlock didn't hurt you?" As I shook my head he suddenly gave me a wide grin. "Quite a night for the quiet English countryside. I've not been prepared for such activity."

Tompkins was watching us; no one was looking at Amaury. He had slipped behind me, behind the constable, picked up the carryall, and dashed for the entrance before we knew it. But there was that other figure. It reached out with a nightstick and tapped Amaury lightly on the side of the head but hard enough to crumple him for a moment. Gavin let out a deep breath.

"Nicely done, Bisley," called Tompkins. " 'E oughtn't to 'ave tried it. We'll be coming." He lowered his voice. "Constable Bisley of Marden Parva, my colleague. Met 'im coming 'ere because of the light. Sigden, 'e's a poacher, told me there was someone 'ere last night. We'll just go halong, miss. Can you manage driving?"

We were ushered out of the keep. Gavin was escorted to Black Peter—he'd ridden with only a bridle, I noted—

and admonished again to meet us at the Priory. Amaury, stumbling on Bisley's arm, was led, still clutching the black bag, to the car and placed firmly in the rear seat with his captor. Constable Tompkins let me drive, but watched carefully for any errors or signs of weakness.

"We'll settle everything at the Priory, miss," he told me comfortably as I swerved into the lane. "Young gentlemen 'ave their differences, I suppose. Per'aps we won't need to charge them?" He looked at me.

In the rising moon I could see him cocking a knowing eye. It wasn't the first time in his jurisdiction that two men had fought over a maid. I said nothing. As I looked back over the past hour I could but feel I had not done all I could—but what had there been to do? I had no answer. I still felt a little muzzy, so I concentrated on the shining whiteness of the moonlit lane and the soft cushions of black made by the hedgerows.

A sound came from the back, and looking in the rear mirror I saw Amaury rub his head, glance at the man beside him and lean forward to tap my shoulder. "Stop, Petra. I must get out a moment."

"There'll be no stopping short of the Priory, miss," ordered Tompkins.

"Petra!" Amaury's voice was sharp, and he raised a fist.

I speeded up. "You can't, Amaury. If you hit a police officer, you're really in trouble. And Mr. Tompkins has your gun."

The hand lowered, and he slumped back in the car. I glanced to one side and thought I saw Black Peter cantering over the fields.

" 'E'll be all right, miss." Tompkins might have been

talking about the weather. "Mr. Gavin could ride with one arm and one leg. Used to ride with wild Indians in Canada, 'e told me. Not the way we do 'ere, of course, but useful.''

As I slowed for the crossroads I heard the hoofbeats through the still air and my heart slowly turned quite over. Gavin had come after me. He'd been told I'd known about the paintings, which must have confirmed his worst suspicions. But once out of that room he'd followed. I wondered if Isabelle had thought of those chimneys at the keep. No matter. He had fought for me, saved me from Amaury. Warmth surrounded me, and I concentrated on driving through white and black.

As I turned into the stableyard I could see lights on in the banqueting hall and heard Black Peter clattering into his stall. The men left the car quickly.

"I must go to the lavatory," Amaury told them.

"Very well, sir. We'll take you to the one downstairs, begging your pardon, miss. We'll bring 'im to the front room."

I eased out of the car. Amaury looked down on me intently. "It didn't work, Cousin, but it will. I'm still going to have you, pictures or no pictures. Wait and see."

My knees went wobbly again so I leaned against the car and watched the three cross to the door. I'd be able to walk in a minute. But I didn't have to. Gavin hurried from the stable, saw the car, and in a flash had swept me up in his arms. It was only natural to rest my head against his chest again and to wish I could go to sleep peacefully. When he asked, "Are you all right?" in a queer jerky voice I could only nod and trust he saw it.

The bright lights in the drawing room made me blink.

I was settled in an armchair near the fireplace, and this time it was Isabelle who brought a damp cloth for my face and Gavin who poured brandy for me to sip.

"Too bad you met the constables and had to come back, Petra," I heard Nico say viciously. "You and Amaury nearly got away. We were about to follow you when you all returned. So I'm waiting. . . . Where are they, Langlade?"

"Just letting Amaury wash up; they'll be here any minute. And it's lucky for you Petra's all right." His voice was without expression.

"I told you they'd come back," Isabelle said gently.

"Too bad you never told me there was a way out of that room as well as in," he shot back.

"You should have realized there would be. And you never asked," Isabelle answered with spirit. "I forgot how it worked. Gavin knew."

I swallowed some brandy and pushed aside the glass and towel. My head felt better. Gavin's hand brushed my shoulder as he and Isabelle moved to the side of my chair. An entrance was expected.

Swathed in a pink silk peignoir trimmed with marabou, a pink boudoir cap made of petals covering her hair, Alexandra swept into the room from the front hall. "What is going on?" she demanded, her eyes bright and alert. "First I hear my door being locked. Then a car leaves, and a horse, and they come back and there are strange noises. Then Isabelle unlocks my door and when I ask her what is happening she just tells me to go back to sleep!"

"I would have if you had," sniffed Eugenia in a lavender housecoat, her hair in curlers (she'd be furious when she remembered that tomorrow) from the rear.

Alexandra's gaze surveyed us all and came to rest on Nico, standing alertly by the table, his right hand in the side pocket of his jacket. "You're responsible," she told him flatly.

Nico smiled unpleasantly. "Go sit there, both of you, and keep quiet." He nodded to the love seat at the end of the room. "I didn't know she had found the key"—he shot a furious look at Isabelle—"and disobeyed orders. Now you're here, I want you under my eye so you can't make trouble."

Alexandra opened her mouth, looked at him, and stalked to the small couch and settled herself bolt upright. Eugenia crouched in the other corner.

"Look here, Nico," began Gavin reasonably, "we can work this out . . ."

"Shut up and don't interfere, or we'll take care of you too." Nico was still watching the door.

There were scufflings and thumps from the back hall, and Nico's mouth twisted. "Dear Amaury seems to be having a little trouble."

He was, for when he was pulled into the room by the two constables his hair was hanging over one eye, his jacket was torn, and the cut on his cheek was bleeding. He was still clutching the carryall.

"Tried to get away, sir," puffed Tompkins. "Tried to knock us both out and grabbed for that gun. I'd moved it to another pocket and we 'eld him." For a peaceable village constable who seldom encountered mayhem and violence I thought Tompkins was doing admirably.

. . . . *189*

"All right, you chaps. Let go," Amaury said heavily. "I won't run."

"No, he won't," Nico agreed softly.

Louis and Manson came in from the hall, Manson looking calmly experienced and not at all like a butler. Just as in a Western, he pulled out two revolvers and pointed one at each constable. "Back with you. The lavatory'll hold you in case you get ideas." He jerked his head. "Frisk them, just to be sure, Louis."

"See 'ere, my man," began Tompkins, shocked. "You can't go lifting a gun from a constable. We don't allow that, nor"—with a glance downward—"carrying them either."

"Don't ask for trouble," Manson advised. "Come along."

Tompkins looked at his face, the guns, and at Gavin. "Better go," Gavin told him gently.

With an outraged snort and a muttered "You wait, my man," Tompkins and Bisley stalked to the hall and clumped down the corridor to the back, followed by the two men with three pistols.

Amaury smiled widely at us all, brushed at his hair, and stepped forward. "Well, dear brother, and what did *you* find?"

Nico's eyes were slits. "Nothing, as you know. The bitch fooled us."

"Not us. You," Amaury crowed. "You're the one she made a fool of, emptying the hypo when you looked at the door."

"Why, you . . ." Nico's whole head seemed to flatten and dart at me as if it would strike like a snake's, but he drew back and turned to Amaury.

Return to Aylforth *190*

"Also I made a mistake in not keeping dear Isabelle with me instead of putting her and Gavin in that place to keep them from interfering, in the nicest way possible. It *was* the fireplace in the ruin—in the cellar?"

Amaury gave a shout of exultant laughter. "Of course. You should have asked me. But you were trying to cut me out. You'd have shoved me in that room, too, if you hadn't been so cocksure. Yes, Petra had found the paintings and hidden them—and here they are." He held up the bag triumphantly.

"Then let's get going," said Manson, from just inside the door.

Nico nodded. "In a moment. Amaury, open up. It's only polite to let them all see what we were after—and what we are taking away." He was pleased with himself again.

"There's no hurry," Amaury protested. "We aren't leaving until tomorrow, anyway. But . . ." Triumph like a toga around him, he strode to the table in the center of the room, opened the carryall, and began to unwrap the parcels. There was not a sound.

As he held up the first Watteau, Alexandra gave an exclamation, "Charming!" and rose.

"Sit down," snapped Nico.

"Young man, remember your manners," Alexandra snapped in return, and kept moving. "You better watch out, or you'll be in trouble."

"I don't trust you." Nico raised his voice. "Go back and keep quiet. Louis and Manson don't care a rap about manners."

Alexandra halted and surved the two men scornfully. "They wouldn't shoot."

"Right," Louis agreed. "Not now. But there's nothing to keep us from hitting you on the head, with this." The revolver spun in his hand until he was holding it by the barrel. "Ask her." He nodded at me. So did Manson.

Alexandra gave me a startled look and moved back to the love seat. Eugenia snuffled.

Oblivious, Amaury was carefully unwrapping the other pictures and now held them up one by one. "There's five hundred thousand pounds for us here," he exulted. "Mother certainly took care of us."

"Quite," drawled Nico. There was sweat on his forehead. "Five hundred thousand pounds at least, and after commissions at that."

Amaury began to wrap the pictures. "I'm going to sleep with these tonight," he laughed. "We can all start for France tomorrow." In his delight he seemed to have forgotten Manson and Louis.

"They'll never let you keep them," I called desperately.

"Don't worry about me, Petra," he said gaily. He was the engaging Amaury again. "You better start your own packing."

I opened my mouth again, but steps were coming through the open front door, and Roger Daintry appeared. "Is anything wrong?" he asked, his eyes on Isabelle. "I was out for a walk—lovely moon—and when I saw all the lights thought I'd better come and see if I could be useful." He looked around inquiringly.

Manson moved behind him and crashed the butt of a revolver on his head. Louis caught him neatly as he sagged, then rolled him against the wall. Isabelle gave a little cry.

"Don't worry, Isabelle. He'll be all right. I'm just sorry he'll be the one to get what I leave." Nico was still relaxed, Isabelle uncomprehending.

Amaury was stowing the paintings in the bag. "I'll help you upstairs, Petra. We'll be leaving early, so you'll have to be ready to come with us."

"She isn't coming." Nico's voice was flat. "She isn't —and you aren't."

Bewildered, Amaury swung toward him. "But we always agreed to share equally, on our portion, after those two men are paid off. Even when I had the pictures by myself I told Petra I'd see you got a share. And the last time we talked you said I could bring Petra along."

"And you believed me, you fool!" He was amused and exultant, too. "You've been a fool all along, you farmer lout. You and that uncle were never meant to share."

Amaury shook his head. "But, Nico . . ."

I jumped from my chair. "You *are* a trusting fool, Amaury. You must have known those two men are professional thieves."

"That's putting it a bit strong. Nico said they were good at finding pictures that were hidden, and knew the right places in London and Paris for us to sell at the best prices."

"And you believed him! All right, but"—I lifted my hand, pointing—"that man you call brother is not Nico."

"Don't be silly. Are you trying to get out of coming with me? You won't. I'm not losing you, *or* the pictures, now."

"She's right." It was Alexandra, rising majestically from the love seat. "That's not Nico. Sloane is back from

London and brought me my mail this evening. The real Nico was taken from Hong Kong harbor but only identified five days ago. I'd asked a friend in Paris to check there. He had a cable and wrote me immediately.''

Amaury lurched around the end of the table. "Is she right? Petra, what do you mean? Why do you say that?''

"Think hard. You said he'd changed in ten years. He doesn't remember things you do. You must have noticed that,'' I began, quite calmly.

Amaury caught Nico's shoulder. "I *have* noticed that. I thought he'd just forgotten . . . he hadn't been around to be reminded.'' His eyes began to glitter again. "Come, now, tell me what color hair did Father's valet, August, have? We were with him often; you'll remember that.''

"Brown,'' spat Nico contemptuously. "Don't always be childish. Petra's getting hysterical.''

"It wasn't brown. He didn't have any hair. He was bald.''

"And''—my voice rose—"he doesn't have a scar on his right shoulder from the hoe, from the time you pushed him down on the blade and it took so many stitches.''

Nico looked honestly bewildered, but knowledge flared in Amaury's eyes as full realization of how he had been tricked and used flooded through him. "I'd put that out of my mind,'' he muttered, "haven't remembered that in years.''

With what seemed like one movement, he whirled Nico around, threw him face down on the floor, straddled him, jerked aside the jacket, and pushed up the shirt. The exposed back was as brown and smooth as I remembered. Amaury let his fingers wander over it for a dreadful moment, then dug in behind the shoulder blade so Nico screamed.

"It was the scar on his back that identified Nico's body." Alexandra's raised voice carried well.

The blond man jumped to his feet and hauled the dark one up to face him. "Why, you filthy bastard," he shouted and went off into French words I did not know. Louis moved nearer the two. Manson, at the door, covered us all.

"Stand back, Amaury," commanded Nico, pale under his tan. With a glance at Louis, Amaury obeyed slowly. "Of course I'm not Nico. We met in Hong Kong a few months ago. We were so alike—and that, dear brother, is one of those strange chances that do happen—that after I'd learned his mannerisms the resemblance was quite useful. He was slipping, had been for some time, and it was easy to get to know him quite well, to get him to talk, endlessly. Once he'd told me his real name he couldn't stop. I have a good memory; it soaked up what he said." He was proud he had fooled us all. "Our organization decided I'd do even better as Nico in France. So I took his ring and was back before the matter of the pictures ever came up. Then, of course, it was obvious what we must do. And by then Nico wasn't much good to anyone—drugs, you know—and he was more useful to us quite dead. The harbor is always handy."

Someone gasped, and Amaury's eyes grew even brighter. "All that time we were together, the questions you asked . . . ?"

"I was filling in what Nico had told me, but not, I see, all the right things. And of course I needed you for cover."

. . . . *195*

"And here . . . when we were alone. You let me talk about Mother and Father. . . ." His rage was growing.

Nico laughed. "You talked with such sentiment! I wouldn't have stopped you. Yes, you were always your mother's darling boy, I could recognize that."

Amaury seemed to swell to twice his size. He leaped across at Nico, pinning his arms and tripping him to the floor. Kneeling, he began to crash the black head against the hearthstone.

Louis was beside him, the revolver raised as a club.

"Look out, Amaury!" I shouted.

He ducked and the blow hit his shoulder, loosening his hold and knocking him off balance. As Nico squirmed free, Amaury was on his feet. Still on the floor, Nico twisted, drew a revolver from his pocket and fired. Amaury's look of fury turned to surprise. He bent forward horridly. As he sagged down, Nico kicked him.

Isabelle screamed. "No, no!" called Alexandra frantically. Beside me I felt Gavin move.

"Stay still, Langlade," cautioned Nico. "We were going to do it on the way to the coast, anyway."

I dropped on my knees beside Amaury. He moved his head, saw me and smiled, sanely and sweetly. "I might have known it was too good to be true . . . the farm . . . and you. Never had any luck. . . . But I could have . . . with you . . . in time." He closed his eyes, then opened them. "Don't let that canaille have the pictures. Get them to Uncle. That's what Mother would want." He stopped. "Mother . . ." He gave a long sigh. Isabelle was sobbing. There were tears in my own eyes. Gavin lifted me back into my chair.

"Mistake to do it here," Louis said tonelessly, "but

he'd have gone for you again. Do we shoot the rest and leave no witnesses?" He was quite matter of fact.

Nico put a hand to his head; his fingers came away bloody. He grimaced and glanced at the floor. "No. This was obviously self-defense, if it ever comes up. But it won't . . . honor of the family . . . and we'll be far away." He glanced around brightly, more pleased with himself than ever, then at me. "But you, Petra, I'm getting square with you. If it hadn't been for you, saying you knew nothing all these days, we'd have found the things and been gone long ago. You thwarted me and tricked me. Nobody can do that without being punished."

I couldn't move as I watched the muzzle of the revolver in his hand rise and point at me.

A second time that night Gavin jumped. His right hand pushed up the gun, his left knocked Nico's head back. There was a shot. Gavin winced. His right hand flicked and was over Nico's on the revolver. Slowly the muzzle rose. Louis was stealing up on the two men, his own gun raised. In a flash I had jumped up, seized the decanter of brandy by the neck and threw it at him. Of course it missed, but my movement and the flash threw him off guard.

"Dangerous thing, leaving front doors open," said a reproving voice from the hall. "Can't tell who'll walk in these days. Alexandra, you're as handsome as ever. Sorry not to have had a chance to talk with you there at Clareham. You wanted me here? What's going on?"

All our faces revolved toward the tall, benign, white-haired gentleman surveying us with the air of a schoolmaster.

"Dudley!" cried Alexandra with more emotion than

I'd ever heard. "Thank God you're here. But why didn't you come sooner?"

Nico and Gavin froze. The hands holding the gun slowly fell, and Nico's left it quickly. Gavin stepped back a pace, the gun hanging at his side. The man in the door glanced at it, at Gavin, nodded and faced Alexandra. "Had to get dressed and round up my men," he said reasonably. "Came as fast as I could, my dear. I must say you sounded uncommonly agitated."

Alexandra nodded. "I was—with cause. I'll tell you. But first you must apprehend these men."

"Must find out what's happened, first. What's this?" He moved into the room and saw Amaury's body and the blood slowly seeping to the beige carpet. Behind him Manson and Louis had gained the door. "Stop," he said. He became quite a different person as he glanced back at them and blew the whistle that hung on a lanyard around his neck. Men appeared in the hall. Manson and Louis, backing with revolvers raised, were caught from behind and disarmed and marched away.

I knew now who the man was: Sir Dudley Campion, Chief Constable of the county. He'd take over. We'd be safe. The tension holding us all relaxed and I smiled toward Gavin, who was standing very quietly. As I did I saw Nico snatch the revolver from Gavin's hand. He raced to the table, seized the carryall, and ran to the empty hall. Gavin was moving, but slowly. At the doorway Nico whirled and fired one shot that crashed into the mirror above me. We could hear him running toward the rear door.

"Get him," I screeched, "he has the paintings!" He *couldn't* be allowed to get away with them.

Return to Aylforth 198

Sir Dudley blew twice. "Don't worry, my dear. We'll get him. Enough men around the house to trap a ferret. Now you can tell me about all this."

A man came and spoke in his ear. "Got him? Good. Just hold him until we can get him to Shaftesbury. But bring in that bag he's carrying. And send in some more men."

Gavin was holding himself upright by one hand on the back of my chair. I touched his arm. His eyes opened. "Petra . . . you're all right?"

"Yes," I assured him. "But . . . you . . . here, sit down." He let me lead him around the chair and urge him into it.

"Bring in the doctor," I heard someone boom as I began to open the bloodstained shirt. The wound was on his left side. I knew enough to know it was well away from his heart.

"You'll be all right," I told him.

"Every intention of being all right," he murmured, eyes closed. As I stepped out of the way, the broken mirror crackled under my shoes. Isabelle was kneeling by Roger, her face white and anxious. I hoped she would take him. She'd make him a good wife, probably all the better because of what loving Nico had done for her. Tompkins and Bisley, having been released, were anxiously explaining to Sir Dudley, I could tell by their expressions. I shuddered and looked away from the cloth that was being put over Amaury. Poor cousin. The Princess would have wanted him to have his farm; he'd deserved it. But she'd be glad the pictures were going back to Montmézay for whatever use the Count would make of them. Beside me a man was bending over Gavin.

"Petra!" Alexandra swept her arms around me and gave me a resounding, fragrant kiss. "I don't really know what you've been up to, but I'm proud of you."

Before I could say anything, Eugenia, still snuffling, pecked my cheek. "I am, too, Pérdita," she managed, but without great conviction. Then she saw Isabelle and Roger and smiled.

"He'll do," said the man in front of Gavin. "Bullet went straight through. Just nicked a rib and lung. He'll be all right in a few days. Campion, send someone to help me get him to bed."

As two men lifted Gavin, two shots came from down the driveway. The Chief Constable's head went up like a pointer's. Alexandra began to speak, but he waved her away. "Made a break, did he? He can't get away. Go to bed now, all of you. I'll be over tomorrow. Doctor, give everyone here something to make them sleep. I'll see Daintry gets home." He bowed to Alexandra and was gone.

Large, impersonal men helped us all to our rooms. I was nearly asleep when I felt a prick on my arm and cried out in alarm. "It's all right," soothed the doctor, and I fell into such a deep sleep that it was noon when I awoke.

13

So it was afternoon when Sir Dudley gathered us in the living room again. Gavin was helped to an armchair by a nondescript middle-aged man Alexandra explained was the new butler she'd found that morning and one whose references were not forged. At that Eugenia looked almost guilty.

"Now, nothing formal," began the C. C. as he settled into another armchair. "We'll have to take depositions later, you understand. But I want to know first what's been happening. Couldn't make head or tail of what you said, my dear." He beamed at Alexandra as if incoherence were a virtue.

"You'd be no clearer about it if you'd found yourself locked in your room and a thief in the house," she pointed out almost coquettishly. "I was so glad I recognized you at Clareham the other afternoon. I knew you'd take care of everything."

"Yes, of course." He positively beamed. "Now, just tell me what you know."

"Not as much as I wish," Alexandra admitted regretfully. "There was nothing tangible, you understand. But I did begin to wonder about this search for paintings by the two cousins and why someone should listen to telephone calls, or a strange man follow Petra's car. And Manson didn't *look* like a butler to me, and he was always around; but Eugenia said he'd come with the *best* references the very day Perkins left without notice. So I could do nothing about that. But out of curiosity I called a friend in Paris and asked him to find out what he could about the Montlucs, and the pictures, though I learned enough about them from another friend in London to explain the search. My Paris friend cabled Hong Kong, as I suggested, again out of curiosity. His inquiry gave the police the clue they needed. Last evening his letter came—there was one son of the Princess in Normandy with the Count; the other was dead in Hong Kong. This time I wondered if there had been a mistake, so I decided to wait until morning and then consult you and Gavin.

"Last night when I found I was locked in I just waited. When Isabelle unlocked the door, I refused to go back to sleep as she suggested and finally dug out of her that Petra and Amaury had disappeared and Nico and Manson had a strange man in the banqueting hall trying to take apart the chimney. Of course I thought of you then and called you on the upstairs phone. After that I came down to see what was happening and Eugenia followed me. I am only sorry I waited about the letter."

"Very clear," Sir Dudley approved. "And don't worry about that letter. Even if we had suspected the man was an impostor, we could not have done anything. Probably all would have happened . . ." He passed over Eugenia and looked at Isabelle.

"I only know a little, at the end." She faltered. "Nico —or whatever his name is—did tell me about his plan to use the drug on Petra. I objected, but he laughed and said it was the only way and would do no harm. Then it seemed to work on her and he was so excited. I thought it was awful. He didn't want me to help him any more. He and the one called Louis made me and Gavin go in the secret room. I had to open the door because Gavin wouldn't, and Louis hit him on the head and they practically threw him inside. It was so black, and I couldn't remember how to get out. But Gavin did when he came to. I'd been thinking, and I told him about the fireplaces at the Marden keep. He found the key Amaury had dropped on the table here and told me to unlock the doors upstairs and just disappeared. So I did, and told Cousin Alexandra what I knew, and came back here. Next Nico came in, and he was furious because they hadn't found anything in the banqueting hall. I reminded him of the keep, too, and he was more furious than ever—and at me. He and Louis went out to get a car and go to the ruin but came right back. Nico was laughing and said the pictures were coming to him without any trouble after all, and sent Louis off to find Manson again. Gavin brought in Petra, and then the others came and things happened, but the others can tell you better than I can." She was sitting very straight and had herself well in hand. I admired her.

"I do seem to have begun at the wrong end," began Sir Dudley, and he wasn't being gallant any more. "Who can start at the beginning for me?"

. . . . *203*

"I'll tell you about the pictures and the young men," Alexandra volunteered, "and Petra can carry on with her story."

I went back to my visit to Nanny. They all watched me, but I was only conscious of Gavin, interested yet aloof, stiff in his chair because of the bandage around his ribs. I found I could quite easily skip all my encounters with him and the incident of Louis. When I mentioned the will and the note in the trunk, I had to go for them. I brought back Winnie himself. He deserved one moment of glory. They all looked amused and understanding as I took out the pin and the stuffing and gave the papers to Sir Dudley.

"Go on," he said cordially.

So I told of my discovery of the pictures and my problem and how Charles had helped, just by coming. I noticed Gavin wasn't smiling any more. I had to mention the visit to the ruins and then my midnight expedition. That horrified the ladies, but Sir Dudley chuckled admiringly; Gavin settled for looking out the window. After that there was only the emptying the hypo and my going with Amaury to the ruin and a mention that Gavin had rescued me—practically from abduction.

"We have the accounts of the constables already," said Sir Dudley. "I think what you ladies have told me fills in everything."

"But Nico, the shots," I protested. "What happened last night?"

The florid face flushed. "Got to admit it. My men slipped. The man got away. I hadn't thought he could. Ran back to your car, Miss Norreys. You'd left in the keys. He started down the lane, turned into the drive, thought it faster, perhaps, and was getting away when Dunham, my aide, shot at the tires. Hit them, too, not bad in that light. The car swerved into one of those oaks.'' He spread his hands.

"Good riddance," said Eugenia roundly, forgetting the charm and gaiety he had brought for a bit to the house. "Who was he really?"

Again the hands spread. "We'll know in a day or so, from the Sûreté or Interpol. Not that it really matters. Now may I see these paintings that have caused so much trouble?''

Where were they? I started up in a panic, but Isabelle was bringing the bag from the table in the hall where it had lain unnoticed all night. Again the pictures were unwrapped and laid on the table.

"Ummm, yes." Sir Dudley stroked his moustache as we all crowded for a last look. "Very nice. You better let me keep them in a safe in Shaftesbury. Who acts for the family? Thetwin? Good sound man. He'll write and arrange . . . everything." He tucked the papers and wrapped pictures into the carryall. "I'll take this immediately. Now you, young man"—he looked hard at Gavin— "I'm seeing you back to bed. Ladies, I recommend lots of tea and a light supper and bed also. Alexandra, my dear, delighted you're in the neighborhood. May I come to call, unofficially, that is?'

The two eyed each other with pleasure, and then he was helping Gavin from the room.

We started to collapse, but the tea revived us. Alexandra was bright-eyed and talkative on all sorts of topics. Eugenia looked slightly crumpled and annoyed. Isabelle was subdued, white and unhappy. Remembering what she had said at the ruin, I was sorrier for her than ever.

When we finished tea I went over and touched her arm. "Come. Let's go out for a walk."

She shrank away, not even glancing at me. "Oh, I couldn't. But thank you."

I picked up her hand. "Come on, I need you." Never before had I said anything like that to Isabelle.

She looked startled but rose. Alexandra watched us thoughtfully. As we started out the door, I heard her say, "Eugenia, you used to like gin rummy. Find the cards, and we'll have a game."

I knew she thought it was her lecture to me in the car that had changed me, but it wasn't only that.

We took the path through the oaks that swung around the orchard and came back through the beeches to the ruins of the monastery. Neither of us spoke, but I felt the tenseness gradually leave the girl beside me.

At the remnant of the wall she leaned against it, then moved away from me. I closed my eyes and could see again the lean man with the high cheekbones and gray eyes. I could have held the picture a long time, happily, but a slight sound made me circle the wall. Isabelle's face was in her hands, and she was crying with deep sobs she tried to stifle. I put my arms around her. After a second of withdrawal she let me hold her while she cried unashamedly. At last she shook her head and straightened and felt for a handkerchief, which neither of us had.

"Use your slip," I advised.

She gulped and did and faced me. "Thank you, Petra." Her voice was unsteady. "I needed that, and I never could have cried in the house. Oh"—she covered her face again—"I've been such a fool. How can I ever face anyone?"

"You weren't a fool," I told her briskly. "Anyone would have been taken in by that charming man he played so well."

She dropped her hands quickly. "Really? Are you sure? But, oh, Petra, I thought he was beginning to care for me, just as I was for him. And then he laughed at me, and was so cruel."

I began to speak carefully. "Forget that part. He was . . . he was exultant. He thought he'd won against us all. I doubt if he was conscious of anything but the pictures. And"—here I crossed my fingers—"I'm not sure he wasn't really beginning to care. When he looked at you it showed."

Her face came up, and there was hope in her eyes. "That's what I thought, of course. But I shouldn't have shown it. You see, I never *have* felt that way before. I never knew anyone like him," she ended, as though that explained everything, and it probably did.

"Well, it's over," I began.

"No. I've been planning how I can get away, where I can visit for a while. I *must*. All of you here saw how I felt about a man who turned out a thief and a murderer."

"I don't believe everyone realized it. And who are we, anyway? Just family. Don't think of him that way; think of him as a most accomplished actor who would have deceived the Pompadour herself, who brought us all a few gay moments." I was beginning to be proud of myself as an adviser to the lovelorn.

. . . . *207*

She brightened a bit more. "That's a nice way to put it. But, Roger . . . he must have noticed."

Here I could uncross my fingers. "Don't worry about him. He probably was only jealous because he saw you enjoying yourself with an attractive man. He'd expect you to. He'd never dream you were serious. And he cares for you—so much—and always has."

"Yes. I suppose you're right." Her smile was sweet. "Dear Roger." She gave me a quick hug. "Petra, I never knew you could be so nice and so . . . so understanding."

"We've never had any chance to be friends since we've grown up." I hugged her back. "Now, hold up your head and act as if it never happened. I don't think your mother will ever mention that man again." I had a feeling Alexandra was giving her that advice right now.

"If she starts I won't let her. And there's Roger."

She was smiling when we returned to the house and looked quite herself as Roger, his own eyes alight, met us by the fountain.

I was the one to feel depressed and a bit lonely as I went into the house by myself.

Next morning Alexandra took me to Shaftesbury to see if anything could be done about my car. Obviously nothing could. I got the papers from the glove compartment and was wondering about the insurance when Sir Dudley arrived, puffing slightly, and so pleased to see us. There would be no problem, he assured me. He'd send an affidavit to Thetwin, who would take care of everything —again. But how about a new car? The three of us whirled to Salisbury in his Rolls. There, while they argued whether Alexandra or the County would pay for a replacement, I chose another Austin, a pale and quite unsuitable robin's egg blue. It was the way I felt. They were both taken aback by the color, but I announced firmly I'd pay for it myself out of the insurance and royalties. That silenced them.

Sir Dudley came back with us for lunch, to see how his patient was doing—just his duty, he said. His visit to Gavin was brief. The young man had to stay in bed another day, he agreed with the doctor on that. When I asked if I could see Gavin for a minute to say "Thank you" he beamed but told me, nicely, the doctor had ordered no visitors yet. Then he and Alexandra settled in the rose garden to exchange gossip of friends and enemies, new and old.

Roger took Isabelle off for a drive. As she watched them leave, Eugenia smiled at me triumphantly. "They make such a handsome couple, and he's very well situated. I was right all along about everything, wasn't I, Pérdita?" Her whole figure exuded smugness as she left me. Somewhere dear Nanny must have been chuckling to herself.

There was no sign of Gavin that day.

By midmorning the next day I was fuming. Susan, who had told me all the village courted her now to hear about the foreigners and their carryings-on, even though she had been locked in at the crisis, reported that Mr. Gavin was up and about in his room. If he was that well, he could have the decency to come out so I could thank him properly and make sure he was all right.

At length I followed my own prescription and went for a walk around the boundaries and back to the ruin.

There I sat down and looked at myself again. What right had I to be angry with Gavin Langlade for not appearing? He'd doubted me from the first—my character, my actions, my motives. But then he'd said only one half of him doubted and the other half wished to believe. But, perversely, I hadn't helped him to believe. At first I'd resented his being in Cousin Aylmer's place, but when that feeling was gone I hadn't recognized the feeling that took its place. If only I had tried to explain everything calmly, but I had to fly off the handle all the time. Now I could see my own uncertainty had done that, but the knowledge was no comfort now. But he'd been unyielding too. Perhaps he didn't really like me at all. My heart sank. That would mean leaving, never watching for his eyes to smile or feel that firm arm around me. I couldn't face that. Pride, reticence, dignity, nothing mattered at the thought of losing Gavin. But would he have me, stubborn Scot that he was? But he'd come to my rescue twice. That must mean something. If he didn't love me, I'd just stay and lay siege to his heart. I did not feel like the prickly, independent Perdita I had known so long. Since he had made no move, I would just have to find out how he felt.

We were finishing luncheon when I was called to the phone in the morning room.

"Peter, darling. I'm delighted. Can't wait to see you. We'll be so happy . . ."—I thought I heard a phone click back in place. Charles was rushing on exuberantly— ". . . to have the story at first hand. I always knew you would do me credit. But you know you need me to look after you."

"What *are* you talking about?" I interrupted.

"Why, the simply fabulous story of your saving the paintings, those simply priceless paintings, from an international gang of thieves. It's fantastic."

"Where'd you hear?"

"Oh, it isn't in the papers, and it won't be. But your Chief Constable told my hosts, confidentially, over dinner last night. When can I see you? What a book! I want every detail."

I began to laugh. "It wasn't like that at all, Charles, really. It was quite unpleasant and frightening."

"Of course, dear. But I knew something would happen. Do let me come tomorrow to tea. Oddly enough, too, I want to see you." His voice became a conspirator's. "As your agent, I have a right to know, darling, and I'll die if I don't."

Still laughing, I agreed to the tea, and went back to the boiled custard. It would be fun to tell Charles, he was always a good audience, and when I had I'd put an end to any ideas he thought he had about us. He wouldn't grieve for long, I was sure.

I forgot him as I went upstairs. If I was going to do anything about Gavin, I must do it before I lost my nerve. But I waited until after I had a nap, to see if I was convinced of what had to be done. When I awoke I was more sure than ever.

I put on my blue linen and took down my silver box and put it in the pocket of my dress. My talisman. Touching it would make me brave. I left the lid ajar so there would be no troubles inside. I marched boldly to his room, knocked once and opened the door. He had been sitting in the big armchair looking out the window and was on his feet by the time I had closed the door.

. . . . *211*

"I'm trespassing again," I began meekly.

"So I see," he agreed in his bleak-Gavin voice.

There was no anger in me. I walked over and stood in front of him. "I wanted to thank you for saving me twice, that night," I said calmly, though my heart began to beat more quickly, and looked up at him.

The skin was tight over his face. He stood stiffly, his right hand on the back of the armchair. "There's no reason to thank me," he answered remotely. "I would have, for anyone." The plaster across his cheekbone showed up whitely against his tan.

"I must apologize to you," he jerked on, "for the— rude things I said to you. But just out of curiosity, I would like to know if you did meet the false Nico in Paris. Except for that one point it seems quite clear you were an innocent victim who just stumbled into things."

I didn't laugh. "You have been rather beastly at times," I agreed. "I went to Paris to arrange for the French production of my first play. Of course I never saw Nico. And the things you said don't matter, now. You couldn't know."

"I've been thinking over . . . everything these past days. I did know, inside. It was all accident on your part. But I wouldn't acknowledge to myself I knew. You behaved so suspiciously! Meeting people, bringing out that box from the wall, going around at night, being hit on the head when there was no one around, how could any man believe the tales you told? They sounded like the wildest fiction. And your story of how you'd forgotten about the letter! Who could believe that? But you worried me all the time because this, well, apparent duplicity didn't go with the charming, intelligent girl you seemed to be. Also, of course, I was jealous and took that out on you too. But I behaved very badly. I'm not explaining myself very well, but I do want to say I'm sorry."

It was a handsome apology. I felt he meant the words, but he had never been more remote. A wall was around him.

"Of course it's all right," I began. "I can understand that everything I did or said looked peculiar and suspicious to you. As you say, things just happened. . . ." I tried a tentative smile. "But you *do* believe me now, so everything's all right. How do you feel? Does the rib hurt? I wanted to come before but the doctor said no visitors allowed."

"There was no need to come. The rib's healing well."

No encouragement there. I tried again. "Life will seem pretty tame, won't it, after all the excitement?"

"Personally, I prefer a tranquil life. But doubtless you will find material for another play for that man to sell for you."

"That man?" I had to stop and think. "Oh, Charles? But I told you I'd never use Aylforth for a story."

"Yes. Charles." We were still, ridiculously, standing facing each other, his hand still gripping the back of the chair. "I'm probably the first to know. I hope you'll be very happy with him."

"What do you *mean?*" His eyes were so bleak my breath caught. "What *are* you talking about?"

"Don't try to deny it. I heard him. I was waiting for a call from Beckham. I knew Charles was in love with you the minute I saw him. And you were so glad to see him. On the phone, during luncheon, he said you'd both be so very happy." He gave a sketch of a bow. "I hope you will be."

"I don't understand. . . ." I was honestly bewildered.

"He obviously does. You must have accepted him."

"*Oh,*" I gasped. It was all so silly I couldn't help laughing.

His face grew harder. "Perhaps I've always been a joke to you both. The strange colonial! But he said that . . ."

I walked away from him. How could he be so blind, and so stubborn? How could I break through the wall, convince him? But suppose he didn't care, didn't feel as I did? He had moved toward the window and presented a rigid back to the room. I must do, say, *something*. And then, on the desk, on the gilded tray that held an ornate inkwell, I saw a white pebble. It was mine, from the abbey wall. I'd smoothed it enough times to know it anywhere. My hand stole into my pocket, touched the dragons, drew out my box. It was still open, but my trouble was too big to put inside. This one I had to take care of myself. But the pebble meant . . . *must* mean. . . . Upstairs I had said that pride, dignity, nothing mattered. I found they didn't.

"Charles means nothing to me," I told the back clearly. "He has been an effective agent and helpful friend, and I hope will continue to be both. But that's all."

Gavin shifted a little to look at me. "But he said . . ." he began stubbornly.

"You should have listened longer. He said 'we,' and he meant where he is staying, would be so happy to have the story about the pictures at first hand. He's coming tomorrow to hear it. Sir Dudley told a dinner party, in confidence, of course. You shouldn't jump to conclusions so quickly."

"How could I help it? He sounded so confident. And I've wanted to see you so much and you hadn't been near me."

I started to say, "You hadn't been near me, either," and put the words aside. I ran and shook his arm a little. "You did want to see me?"

"Of course I did. I wanted to ask you to forgive me. Can you, after a while?" He was anxious; the wall was almost down.

"But there's more than that. See." I made him turn and pointed to the desk. "My white pebble. You got it and brought it here. And, here"—I pulled out my box—"I brought this with me to give me courage." I put it on the desk by the pebble. "They belong together."

Suddenly he laughed, happily. "Oh, Petra, you darling. I'm the one who needs the courage after the way I behaved. I've thought so much these two days. I know now I've loved you since we went for that drive together. Can you forgive me for not knowing more quickly? I didn't realize until I saw you lying there on the couch, helpless, white, frightened and trying not to show it, and Nico threatening you. I was so afraid he'd hurt you I couldn't even look at you. I didn't dare move."

There was no longer any wall. I reached up and stroked his cheek. "But you moved fast enough later," I reminded him. "Twice. And saved me both times."

His arm went around me and he bent his head. "Will those two times make up for everything else? Do you forgive me, now? I thought I might have to wait weeks

· · · ·   *215*

before you'd even speak to me. Oh, love, is it going to be all right? I'll make you happy, always, I swear.''

I put my arms around his neck and looked at him squarely. A glow was spreading through me. ''Are you proposing to me, Gavin?''

His arm tightened. ''I am. Here and now. I've been planning . . . I was going to wait, give you time. . . . Then I heard that man. Gave me the worst three hours of my life. Kept remembering all I'd said to make you dislike me. But you don't have to answer, now, Petra. I want you to be *sure*.'' He was anxious again.

''But I *am* sure. Here and now, I accept you. I know I couldn't live without you.''

His eyes were bright, his laugh joyous. ''Oh, my little love. I didn't dare hope.'' His kiss dizzied me, and as I answered it I could feel he was shaken also.

When we drew apart I saw the silver box. I could close it now, forever, with no troubles inside it. Oh, who wouldn't have troubles with such a stiff-necked man, but they'd be ones to solve with joy and love, not to shut up in secret. Perhaps the box could hold the pebble . . . the two talismans together. . . . And as I raised my face to his, I knew I'd never be alone, or lost, or doubted, again.